"Can I have your number?"

Heat rushed up over Jess's face. Was he really about to ask her out? After the argument they'd just had? Surely not.

"That way I can find a good time to look at the data and to follow up regarding the individual meeting."

Of course…

She swallowed hard. As much as she didn't want to date, she wasn't completely immune to the charms of a handsome man. Hopefully, he hadn't caught her moment of girlish stupidity at thinking that he might be flirting with her. Beckett grinned widely when she glanced up at him, though.

Great.

The blush would have been bright on her pale face. He wouldn't have missed it. Now he would think she was interested in him. She rattled off her number, stumbling twice over the numerals because she was still so darn shaken. *That's what happens when you barely speak to men*, she thought. *You get so out of practice that you don't know what flirting even is!* When her phone buzzed in her pocket, she nearly jumped out of her skin.

Dear Reader,

Sometimes when you meet "the one," the timing is off. Or you convince yourself that the timing is off—as the heroine of this book, Jessamine, has done. But love finds a way, doesn't it? Love overrules your objections and sails clear over the hurdles you erect around your heart. Beckett had more than a few obstacles to get around when fighting for his chance to love Jess—including a tornado!

A very long time ago now, a tornado hit my school and it partially collapsed. I've wanted to use some of that experience in a story for ages, but it needed to be the right time and the right characters. I finally found that story.

Please enjoy, and happy reading!

Allie

SAVING THE SINGLE MOM'S HEART

———

ALLIE KINCHELOE

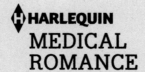

HARLEQUIN

MEDICAL
ROMANCE

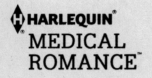

HARLEQUIN®
MEDICAL
ROMANCE™

Recycling programs
for this product may
not exist in your area.

ISBN-13: 978-1-335-73724-3

Saving the Single Mom's Heart

Copyright © 2022 by Allie Kincheloe

For questions and comments about the quality of this book,
please contact us at CustomerService@Harlequin.com.

Harlequin Enterprises ULC
22 Adelaide St. West, 41st Floor
Toronto, Ontario M5H 4E3, Canada
www.Harlequin.com

Printed in U.S.A.

Allie Kincheloe has been writing stories as long as she can remember, and somehow, they always become romances. Always a Kentucky girl at heart, she now lives in Tennessee with her husband, children and a growing menagerie of pets. Visit her on Twitter: @alliekauthor.

Books by Allie Kincheloe

Harlequin Medical Romance

The Christmas Project
Winter Nights with the Single Dad

Heart Surgeon's Second Chance
A Nurse, a Surgeon, a Christmas Engagement
Reunited with Doctor Devereaux

Visit the Author Profile page at Harlequin.com.

For my family. Like the characters in this book,
things haven't been easy for us.
But we've made it through. I love you.

CHAPTER ONE

"YOU KNOW WHAT would be great? If I had a dad to pick me up from school."

Jess Daniels glanced up at her son in the rearview mirror and tried not to sigh at the familiar topic of conversation. Mason was relentless with his idea that she needed a man in her life, if only to be his dad. "Miss Freya says no one should be alone as much as you are. Miss Freya says that she works all the time and she still goes to see her friends more than you do. Do you have any friends besides Miss Freya?"

"I have friends, Mason." She just didn't see them as much as any of her friends would have liked. But that came with the whole single mom situation, didn't it? Getting a sitter was hard and expensive.

"Do you know how to get a boyfriend? Miss Freya says if I want a dad, then we gotta find you a boyfriend first. But I've never seen you have a boyfriend, so you might have to take lessons or something. Like when I go to karate lessons."

"Boyfriend lessons?" Jess snorted.

That boy was determined he needed a dad, and soon. And as long as the man knew how to play video games and throw a ball, then her son wasn't too choosy. From the time he was old enough to realize that most kids had a dad somewhere in their lives, Mason had been asking questions about his own father. Questions that were proving harder to answer now that he was no longer content with the explanation that his father had passed away before he was born. But she sure wasn't ready for him to learn the truth about his paternity.

She'd have to have another talk with Freya about encouraging Mason like this. Why couldn't anyone understand that Jess wanted to be alone? She *might* have let Freya believe that her lingering love for Mason's dad kept her from dating since it gave her a reprieve from being set up. Some things were harder to get over than grief though, like broken trust. It had been almost eight years since she'd lost Clint, and it might be another eight before she could bring herself to trust another man. She got so tired of hearing about how she really needed to just be brave and put herself out there. One heartbreak didn't mean all men were all bad. Take a chance on love. Have faith.

Meh.

The potential positives didn't outweigh the probable negatives. She was fine being single. *Mostly.*

"There's a Doughnuts with Dad thing at school next week," Mason informed her. "And I can't go because I don't have a dad."

"Tone down the dramatics. You know I'm allowed to go with you instead." She'd gone to the Muffins with Mom and the Fruit Cups and Family events with him already—why not a doughnut day? She hated the designated days for each parent. It was unfair to the kids who didn't have an intact traditional family.

"It's not the same," Mason huffed. "I need a dad."

"If we ever see a dad store, I'll be sure to pick one up."

"Ha-ha." The kid didn't appreciate Jess's sarcasm. "I'm not going to fall for that. I'm not five anymore. Hey, what do all those lights mean?"

Jess swallowed hard as she took in all the icons illuminated on the gauge cluster of her aging sedan. A lot of money for repairs she just didn't have at the moment, that's what they meant. Her chest tightened as she glanced into the rearview mirror and changed lanes before pulling the car off onto the shoulder.

"The car seems to be having some trouble."

"What about my ice cream?"

"Mason, honey, we will get your ice cream as soon as we can." The upbeat tone she spoke with only partially masked her worries—hopefully enough that Mason wouldn't catch on. She thanked her lucky stars she was able to get the car out of traffic and that her son's biggest worry was that he might not get ice cream.

After easing the car to a stop, she put it in Park. The faintest whisp of smoke curled up from under the corner of the hood. That could not be a good sign. Would this finally be the repair that crossed over the value of her little car? Jess rubbed a hand over the steering wheel and sent up a little prayer that the car would be fixable. A new one was so not in the budget right now.

"Stay here while I see how bad this is." She looked over her shoulder to her seven-year-old. "Do not get out of this car until I tell you it's okay."

He nodded, but she'd have to keep a close eye on him. Mason could get into trouble faster than she could blink. She dug her cell phone out of her purse and handed it to him. That should keep him occupied and safe for a few moments, at least.

"Call Freya and ask her to come get us. Tell her we're on the interstate coming home from baseball. Okay?"

At his nod, she popped the hood and, after checking for traffic, stepped out of the car. She lifted the hood and stared at the smoking engine. She knew nothing about cars, but still, she had to look. What was she going to do?

Whatever it was, it wouldn't be fixing this car by herself; that was for sure.

Rather than step back into traffic, she moved to the passenger side of the car. She opened the front door and tried to reassure Mason that everything was fine. "It's going to be okay. Is Freya coming?"

"She said she's got a meeting with the hospital mister tater, and she can't come till after." Mason handed the phone back to Jess with very little concern for what Freya's words meant.

"The hospital administrator?"

"Yeah, that." Mason shrugged. "Whatever."

Jess wanted to laugh at how completely unbothered Mason was about his vocabulary mixup. She envied the confidence her son showed sometimes, how he could make a mistake and just brush it off and move on. He didn't dwell on it like she would. Her mind liked to remember embarrassments from her childhood like they were current events. And the mistakes she'd made as an adult? Those were practically on a reel in her mind, circling through anytime she found herself in similar scenarios.

"Well, let's see if we can get the tow truck out here soon." She looked up the number for the repair garage, although she should have it memorized or saved in her phone given how frequently she used it. She gave them the location and the mechanic confirmed they'd send the truck out but it might be a while. She thanked the man and hung up the phone.

"Gonna be here a while?" Mason groaned.

"That obvious?" She reached back and brushed a lock of hair away from his eyes.

"It's always a while when we gotta wait for the tow truck." He shrugged. "Wanna play a game?"

CHAPTER TWO

BECKETT WILDER PULLED UP behind the black sedan with the hood raised. He'd driven by the first time and then his EMT instincts had kicked in. Leaving someone stranded on the side of the road went against the fiber of his being, so he'd looped around at the next opportunity. He flicked his emergency flashers on to warn passing drivers to be cautious. When there was a gap in traffic, he climbed from the cab and approached on the passenger side.

A woman climbed out of the car. She looked to be a few years older than him, maybe. Her blond hair was in a ponytail, and she wore a Woodvale Woodchucks baseball T-shirt. "Thanks for stopping but I've already called for a tow."

"How long until they get here?" Unless things had changed since he'd left home, Woodvale had a single tow truck and the owner tended to take his slow, sweet time about getting his job done.

She hesitated before answering. "A couple hours."

That wouldn't do. He couldn't leave her out here for hours. As an EMT, he'd seen more than his share of roadside accidents. A stalled car or a flat tire led to someone getting hit more than it really should. The caution those experiences instilled in him, combined with the knowledge that his own sister had died not three miles down this very same road, made him anxious to get her out of here.

"You alone?" A glimmer of fear sparked in her green eyes, and he wanted to kick himself for not introducing himself or doing something to put her at ease. A lone woman on the side of the highway being approached by a strange man? Of course she'd be concerned. "I'm Beckett, by the way. When I'm not being a bonehead and scaring the people that I'm trying to help, I work as an EMT."

His attempt at humor during his introduction fell flat. She didn't even crack a smile. Her eyes narrowed as she said, "I know all of the EMTs here and you aren't one of them."

"You're right. I don't work here in Woodvale." He pulled his wallet out of his pocket and flipped it open to his driver's license. "I did grow up here though. You may know my parents, Richard and Elaine Wilder?"

Tension left her shoulders and she visibly relaxed as she read his name on his identification. One pro of being the son of the richest couple in town was name recognition. At least, it was a pro in this instance. That same recognition had forced him to leave town to get enough anonymity to grow his career as an EMT on his own terms.

"You look like your dad," she finally acknowledged.

"I hear that a lot. So, now that you've verified that I'm not a serial killer or something, can I give you a ride home?" His eyes flickered to the small cross set back away from the highway. His sister had a similar cross marking the spot where she had breathed her final moments. "This isn't the safest spot to be sitting."

She glanced over to the little white marker placed near the tree line. "The tow truck said it would be a while and to leave the keys under the front mat if we left."

"Then let's get you somewhere safe."

Her teeth worried her lower lip as she considered his offer. The wind picked up and blew her hair around her face. She shoved it back with an impatient hand. "I really appreciate you doing this. Did I introduce myself? I don't think I did. I'm Jess Daniels."

"It's nice to meet you, Jess. But I wish it were under better conditions."

She shrugged before she opened the back door. A little blond boy climbed out of the back wearing a Woodchucks baseball uniform. The little boy waved happily, and Jess kept a firm grip on him as she steered him toward the truck. "Come on, sweetie. Mason, this is Mr. Wilder. He is going to give us a ride."

"Hi, Mason." Beckett opened the back door. "He needs a booster seat, right?"

"Yeah, I just wanted to make sure he was inside a vehicle before I turned my back long enough to unclip it."

"I got it." He hurried over to the car and made quick work of disconnecting the child seat. It had been the glimpse of that seat in the back of the broken-down sedan that had really driven home the need for him to stop and offer his assistance. He carried it over and had it installed in his own vehicle before she could offer to try to do it herself.

When her son climbed up into the seat, she had him buckled in quickly. "Thank you," she said softly as she closed the back door. "I really do appreciate you stopping. I'm sure you had better things to do."

"Nothing is more important than making sure the two of you are safe. Got it?" Beckett's words were sincere. He never wanted another family to go through the pain of losing a loved one on the side of this highway like he had. Impulsively, he reached out and touched her hand. Their fingers tangled for a moment, and his heartrate quickened when she didn't instantly pull away. The shy smile she gave him made him want to pull her in close, but then the shutters in her eyes slammed closed and she yanked her hand away like he'd burned her. The action made him curious, but he didn't push. He opened the passenger door and gestured for her to get in. "In you get."

He waited for a break in traffic before walking around. She avoided eye contact when he climbed into the cab. She gave off a very independent vibe. He liked that in a woman, but Jess had walls built up around her the size of Fort Knox.

If circumstances were different, he might try to flirt, to see if they could have some fun together. Jess was exactly his type in every way except for one key factor: she was a mom. Long-term relationships weren't in his wheelhouse. He dated, frequently, but never for more than a few months at a time. Once things started getting serious, he was out. Kids in the mix were a major nope from him.

As he pulled back onto the road, he asked, "Do you see those clouds coming in? They're saying we're in for some rough storms, maybe even some flash flooding."

Weather was neutral, unoffensive. Merely a small-talk topic that would hopefully distract him. He picked a subject that had nothing to do with either of them. The woman had so much tension after his simple touch that he thought better of flirting with her. He was only in town for six months, and she might need that much time to thaw the ice around her heart. Too much work for a short-term thing.

"I'd heard that. Mason was really glad that it didn't come in before his game."

Baseball was another solidly neutral topic, one that they could include her kid in. "I bet. Nothing worse than being excited to play and then have it called for lightning. Is this your first year playing?"

"I played last year too." Mason squirmed in the backseat, catching Beckett's eye. A pained expression crossed his face. "I like baseball."

"You okay, buddy?"

"I need to go to the bathroom really bad!" Mason cried in response.

Beckett stepped a little harder on the gas. The last thing he wanted was for that kid to have an accident in the backseat of his truck. He took the Woodvale exit, sighing when he passed the pair of crosses there. Passing that spot still sent an ache through his chest.

"Someone you knew?" Her voice was soft, cautious even, like she knew she might be treading on sensitive ground.

"My sister."

"I'm sorry for your loss. It's hard to lose a loved one." Experience tinged her voice.

"I miss her every day." Beckett turned at the light at the end of the ramp. Memories of his sister flooded into his mind. "Sloane was… spoiled. She was materialistic and thought she was better than most everyone. But she got me in ways that my dad never could. She could translate for us into language that we could each understand. Some days I still can't fathom that I'll never see her again."

"I feel the same way about my parents. It's been four years since I lost my mom, and I still pick up my phone to call sometimes before I remember that I can't."

"It's supposed to get better with time, or so they say." He pulled the truck to a stop in front of the gas station. "I'll wait here if you want to run him in to the bathroom."

"Thanks," Jess murmured. She got out and took Mason inside.

Beckett leaned his head on the steering wheel and tried to quiet the riot of emotions that talking about his sister always stirred up. Eight years and it still hadn't gotten any easier to be in this town. To be so close to where his sister lay dying on the side of the interstate while the town's sole ambulance took the other driver in because his wounds were more visible. Visible, but not as serious as the internal bleeding that Sloane and her fiancé had suffered.

He let out a ragged breath. He'd get this town the services they needed and then he'd be gone. Away from all the painful memories that surrounded him on every corner. He'd be counting down the days until he could get back to Lexington and the career he had waiting for him there.

Jess and her son came back out to the car, and he could tell by the way her expression shifted that she was misreading his mood. He tried to clear the frustration from his face, but it was too late. She'd already gotten the wrong opinion.

"I'm sorry we bothered you. If you could just drop us off, we live just a few blocks away."

"But, Mommy, what about my ice cream?" There was a tone of urgency, sort of a "how dare you forget?" in Mason's question.

She made sure Mason was buckled in properly before climbing back into the front seat. She didn't once make eye contact with Beckett. "Mommy will have to get you ice cream another day. We can't keep Mr. Wilder any longer than we already have."

Mason huffed. "But you promised!"

"I'm sorry. I didn't know when I promised that the car was going to die. I'll make it up to you once the car gets fixed." Her expression held no trace of emotion. "I think we have some popsicles at home."

"It's not the same."

Beckett looked up in the rearview mirror. Mason had his arms crossed over his chest, lips poked out in a classic pout. Poor kid. He'd had a morning and just wanted to have his promised treat. Beckett remembered all too well the feeling of having a reward snatched away after the fact. In his case, usually because his dad found something more urgent to do.

"We live just up on Sycamore," Jess directed him, ignoring the sulking child in the backseat.

When he glanced Jess's way, he caught the resignation on her face. Having to accept help from a stranger had probably been a hit to her pride, and that was something she needed. Asking for something like ice cream—not a necessity—seemed out of character, at least as much as he could judge after such a short acquaintance. She was simply trying to make it through the day with a few shreds of dignity left.

Instead of turning right on Sycamore, he

drove past and turned into the lot of the ice-cream parlor. He could make this day a little better for them by helping her keep her word to her son.

She put up a token protest. "You don't have to do this."

"A promise is a promise." He shrugged. "It's maybe an hour out of my day. And ice cream sounds good."

The smile she flashed him made it worth it. "Mason, you need to say thank you to Mr. Wilder. I wasn't going to ask him for yet another favor, but he seems to be as determined as you to get that ice cream."

"Hey, us ballplayers gotta stick together," he said, tugging on the brim of Mason's hat as they walked toward the door.

"You play baseball?" A look of awe crossed Mason's face. "My coach this year is Colby's dad and he never played baseball. We do coach pitch, and he's awful."

"Mason," Jess warned, "be nice."

Mason rolled his eyes and continued, "He tries, but he throws like a girl."

"Mason!"

"I know, I know, I shouldn't say throws like a girl because sometimes girls can actually throw." Mason gave Beckett a look that said, *Moms just don't understand.*

"Totally get that." Beckett tried really hard not to laugh. He hadn't been around kids much, but this one was cracking him up. Between the boy's actual comments, and the full range of expressions that the kid was bringing out on Jess's face, Beckett was having a hard time keeping the laughter in. He hadn't been this amused in a long time.

Mason gave him a calculating look. "We could really use a coach that knows how to play."

"Mason!" Jess hissed the boy's name out, her cheeks pinkening up.

Mason shrugged before running up to the counter to check out all the flavors, leaving Beckett and Jess alone for the moment. Silence stretched between them while Beckett scrambled for a neutral topic of conversation that might pull some of the embarrassed color out of Jess's face.

"I would never…" She paused to take a deep breath. "I swear I did *not* put him up to recruiting you—or anyone else—to coach."

Beckett brushed it off. Kids were known for having no filter, right? And he could tell that she hadn't put Mason up to asking. "No need to apologize. Let him enjoy his ice cream."

"Thank you for this, and for coming to our

rescue." She reached out and touched his wrist. A prickle of awareness raced up his arm from the point of contact. "But don't let him talk you into anything. I really appreciate all this, but I don't want you to spend any more time than necessary with him."

"What?" Beckett snorted. He pulled his hand away from her touch, stuffing it in his pocket. He'd tried to make a nice gesture, and all it got him was accusations. The desire to defend himself rose up, but he had no idea what he'd done to give her the impression that he might do something to her kid. "You can't think I'm a bad influence on him."

"I never said that." She sighed. "I'm making this worse. Bear with me for a second. You don't live here, right?"

He shook his head slowly. What did that have to do with anything?

"Are you planning to move here?"

"No way." This town would be in his rear-view the moment it was feasible. Once his dad's cancer treatments and this urgent project his dad had called him home for were finished, he had every intention of going back to his job.

"Then it's not fair to let him get attached to you and leave. He doesn't need that." She flashed him a sad smile. "He's...more fragile than he seems."

"Got it." He might be mistaken, but he thought maybe she was warning him that her own heart was fragile too.

CHAPTER THREE

JESS BIT HER LIP. Had she hurt Beckett's feelings? Getting attached to a man and then losing him could only hurt Mason. Men lost interest fast. She'd learned that the hard way. It was better for all of them if they kept their distance and then she could protect Mason from the same hardships that she'd faced.

Beckett moved away from her, his expression grim. He stood next to Mason at the ice cream counter. When he bent down to talk to Mason, his face softened into genuine interest at whatever Mason was jabbering about.

Jess took several deep, slow breaths. It was one day. It would be okay. Mason couldn't get too attached over a single order of ice cream, right? Even as the thought crossed her mind, she could see the hero worship in her son's eyes as he stared up at Beckett. And she could see why—not only had Beckett literally rescued them from the side of the road, but he'd brought them to get ice cream and he knew about baseball. The only way he could get more awesome would be if he wanted to go to the arcade too—at least according to Mason.

She'd have to be extra vigilant at keeping them apart. Really though, there was no reason for the two of them to be together after today. That realization went a long way toward calming her nerves.

One hour.

Maybe even less.

She just needed to keep them from bonding too much over the next hour. Then she could get back to her lonely life. No, her *normal* life. She wasn't lonely. She had Mason and Freya. She had a few other friends. And work, of course.

Pathetic.

She sighed.

"Don't have your flavor?" Beckett asked, his eyebrow arched. The way he looked at her made the question feel like it wasn't about ice cream at all. Heat crept up into her face as they made eye contact. If she were looking for a man, Beckett would definitely be her "flavor." Tall, dark hair and strong. Oh, he would be any woman's flavor…

Jess looked away quickly, angry at herself for reacting to Beckett's gaze. This was not who she was. Men were not on her menu, especially not men who didn't even live in her town. She ordered a scoop of chocolate without looking at the other options.

She kept a running commentary in her head of all the reasons why she needed to keep her distance from Beckett.

He's the enemy, Jess. He'll love you and leave you, just like Clint did. His time in Woodvale has a clear expiration date. Don't forget that.

Beckett insisted on paying for the ice cream, swiping his card before she could even pull her wallet out of her purse. "Come on, it's less than ten bucks. Don't worry about it."

She would though. Worry about it, that was.

Because one day, he might want to even the score. And she was currently down by two. She murmured a thanks and they headed out to one of the covered tables on the patio to eat their treats. The sunlight peeked through the clouds for the moment and the warmth of the spring day contrasted nicely with the cold ice cream. In another situation, Jess would enjoy soaking up a little sun after the chill of winter had passed, but that was proving hard for her with Beckett nearby. Beckett was the first man since Clint that she'd been this attracted to, and it wasn't sitting well with her.

Thankfully, Mason's chatter kept an awkward silence from developing. That child never ran out of things to say, and the sugar rush from the ice cream kept that running commentary coming at a fast clip for a while. For once, Jess was glad that her little boy could happily chat with anyone about anything.

Even so, there was a tension at the table. When Beckett stretched his leg out and it brushed hers, it pulled the air from her chest. She gasped for breath and tucked her legs back up under her seat tightly. The contact should have felt casual—*should* being the operative word. It was anything but casual.

"Sorry." He voiced the apology, but based on the look in his eyes, he didn't mean it. His gaze held a playful mischief that belied his words. He was flirting with her!

She gave him a little shake of her head.

His eyes twinkled, but he turned his attention back to Mason's recap of that morning's game. Every play was described in excruciating detail, complete with actions and sound effects.

Jess swirled the chocolate ice cream around in the dish with her spoon. The look on Mason's face sent all kinds of red flags up. The warnings were lighting up like all the icons on her gauge cluster had a short while ago. She wanted to snatch the melting ice cream away from Mason and insist that Beckett drive them home immediately. She wanted to put some much-needed space between them. And then she could get back to the way she liked things—where she was alone. If she didn't let anyone close, then her heart—and more importantly Mason's heart—couldn't be in danger.

People always said she shouldn't be alone—Mason, her mom before she'd passed away, Freya. They loved to point out how long it had been since she dated. She usually shut that down hard, but occasionally, the longings for someone to share her life with rose up from somewhere deep. The long, hazy summer nights were the hardest. That's when she remembered walking along the lake at sunset with a man she loved at her side. When she missed the feel of a strong pair of arms around her, holding her until the sun rose.

Then a swift recap of the past would put that silly notion back in the locked box at the bottom of her heart where it belonged. No, while being a single mom was tough, dating was not something she could do. Trust enough to let someone in? Nope. That wasn't gonna happen again. Not after the third-degree burns Clint had given her.

But she hadn't seen Mason this happy in a long time. He was reveling in the masculine attention Beckett was providing. Just having a man listen to his chatter and share in his conversation had put a light in her son's eyes. So, despite her reservations, she sat back and let the conversation play out while the ice cream in front of her melted.

She hated that giving her son what he needed meant allowing someone else to help. Since the day the child was born, it had been the two of them against the world. With Clint gone, Mason had only been hers. Sharing him was not something she was good at. It chafed to know that what he needed most right now was a man.

If she'd had a motto these last seven years, it would have been that "love was nice while it lasted, but the pain it causes is not worth the risk." She'd thought she'd found the type of love her parents had when she met Clint. She'd given herself over to him—mind, body and soul. After having her heart ripped out and stomped on, she'd kept anyone of the male persuasion as far away as possible. Had keeping her heart wrapped up tight behind layers of emotional bubble wrap been the right thing? For herself, absolutely. For Mason? Now she was starting to wonder.

Some days, finding Mason a dad sounded like a good idea. Usually on the days when she'd been on her feet for twelve hours straight, when a protein bar served as the closest thing she'd had to lunch or the space between paydays got a bit too stretched out for comfort...

They did all right though. The bills were paid. They had plenty of food and a solid roof over their heads. It was hard, yes, but she held her head high with pride at all that she had done on her own. Mason had everything he needed and a few things he wanted.

Except a dad. Had she underestimated how important that was to a little boy's well-being?

"Are you ready?" Beckett's deep voice interrupted her thoughts.

"Yes, sorry. I think I zoned out." She'd gone so far into her thoughts that she was questioning years of decisions. That wasn't good. "Thanks again," she said, shooting him a grateful smile.

"No problem." He grabbed a napkin and wiped at Mason's face. "Little dude, I think you're wearing as much of this ice cream as you consumed."

"Do you have kids?" Mason asked.

"Mason…" Jess winced at the bald question, sure she knew where this was going. She hoped to cut it off before Mason took it all the way. "I'm sorry, Beckett. Someone has forgotten his manners."

Beckett chuckled. "It's fine. And no, I don't have kids. My mom really wants me to though. She's been on my case for a while now."

"I think you'd be a good dad," Mason said

softly, flinging himself into Beckett's chest. "I wish I had a dad like you."

Oh, way to lay it on thick, kid. Mason usually didn't take to people that quickly, but in such a short time he'd effortlessly bonded with Beckett. Her fears were coming to life, right before her eyes. Attachments could only end in pain when they were severed. Was there any way this situation could get worse?

CHAPTER FOUR

ON MONDAY MORNING, the special committee members slowly trickled past Beckett and into the conference room to join Freya. He'd been happy to see at least one friendly face in his old buddy from high school. Tugging at the tie around his neck, Beckett only managed to tighten it and make it feel more like a torture device. It had never been his dream to wear designer suits or represent his family foundation, but here he stood. He had to take several deep breaths before his nerves were calm enough for him to walk through the door himself.

Returning to Woodvale hadn't even been his idea. This town held a lot of hurt and a lot of sad memories for him, but he was a dutiful son. When the call came that his father needed his help, what else could he do but move home and step up to the plate? He just wished it didn't feel like that plate sat on unstable ground.

When Beckett entered the space, he noted

with surprise that the woman he'd picked up on Saturday was now seated across the conference room table from the empty seat his father had reserved for him. So she worked at the hospital? Well, that would explain why she'd known he wasn't an EMT here. He stole a glance at her while his father was quietly conversing with someone.

She flicked her long braid over her shoulder and returned his gaze boldly. When he didn't look away, she raised a single brow at him and gave her head a bit of a shake. So far, she was the one challenge this town held that he'd willingly take on—if she didn't have a kid. He had a feeling that any relationship Jess got involved in would need to have that promise of happily-ever-after and that wasn't what he was about. Still, he couldn't deny that seeing her here had unsettled him.

And anyway, dating in Woodvale came with its own complications. The burden to carry on the family name was building, added to by his mother's not so subtle jabs. He was their only hope now that Sloane was gone, after all. She didn't stop the guilt trip there though. No, over breakfast this morning, she'd tossed in the suggestion that if he didn't start a family soon his father might not be around to meet any potential grandkids.

So, no pressure. No pressure at all.

Did he even see himself as the white picket fence type? As a dad?

That was something he wasn't so sure about. He liked kids well enough, when they weren't his and he didn't have to handle the discipline and misbehaviors. Maybe, someday, he might decide to take that plunge, but when—if—he got married, it would be on his terms.

"Are we ready to begin then?" his dad asked.

Beckett sat up straighter. His heart raced even though he knew what his father was about to say. Still, the idea had been abstract before—announcing it to a room full of people would make it far more real. And harder to ignore.

"I'm not sure I need to introduce myself, but on the off chance I haven't met some of you, I'm Richard Wilder. You may have heard rumors to this effect, but the Wilder Foundation has decided to make a rather large donation to Woodvale Memorial."

The room broke into an excited murmur. The people around the table perked up. Gone were the resigned expressions. They'd been replaced by ones of hope. Tentative in a few cases, but still far more optimistic than before the announcement. Jess's entire countenance had brightened and the change in her was striking.

For once, Beckett felt like his family's money might do something that truly helped people.

His dad held up a hand, asking for silence. When the room quieted, he continued, "Now, before you get too excited, much of the money has been earmarked for a cancer center. I have had the misfortune of finding out the hard way that Woodvale has no resources for someone with cancer. None. It's unacceptable for residents of our growing community to have to travel two hours each way for chemotherapy or radiation treatments."

Several people at the table nodded. How many of them had experienced firsthand, through themselves or a family member, exactly how lacking the health care in Woodvale was? Beckett rubbed his thumb against the face of his watch—the last gift his sister had ever given him. Woodvale's lack of proper ambulances had taken Sloane from them, and he wasn't sure he'd ever forgive this town for that.

And now this small town's medical limitations were causing his dad problems as well. Cancer didn't discriminate based on how close someone was to a treatment facility. His dad was lucky enough to have the resources to make those drives to get the care needed. Many of the poorer residents might not.

"With that said, I had them set up this special committee so that we can look at what other areas of our healthcare system are lacking. Through this group and individual meetings with the representatives of each department, the Wilder Foundation will look at funding requests and see how many we can grant."

The excited chatter picked up in volume.

His dad cleared his throat. "My son, Beckett, will be heading this project for the Wilder Foundation. He's the contact for all proposals and requests. He's the one you need to woo to your side."

Beckett stood, though he couldn't help but notice Jess's reaction to that news. She did not look happy in the least. He gave the little spiel he'd prepared about how they should ask for big-ticket items, not little things. "In the next two weeks, I'd like to meet with each of you individually prior to the submission of your proposals. The final decisions on funding will be made shortly after I've had time to review each request. I'm only in Woodvale for the next six months, so everything will be completed within that time frame."

"What are the individual appointments for?"

Beckett turned his attention to the older man who'd asked the question. "Those meetings will be for you to show me around your departments. Explain your needs. Let me see firsthand what your department means to this community and help me understand how the Wilder Foundation can help you help others. As you write your proposals, put the emphasis on how the project benefits the community as a whole, rather than only a select few."

"Can't you just divide the money up equally among the remaining departments and let us decide how the money should be spent?" Jess leaned forward, elbows on the table. "It would be faster and give us more flexibility in how it is used. And it wouldn't take time out of our already busy days to meet with you."

"We could, yes. But we prefer to make directed donations with specific purposes that can make the biggest impact, and dividing the money between departments doesn't address that." He leaned forward too, hands on the surface of the table. "If you prefer to put in a general request for money, you can certainly skip the individual meetings and send in an unspecified proposal. However, I will prioritize the proposals from departments that have proven to me that they have the greatest needs for funding and shown me how they will make the best and most efficient use of the funds."

He could hear Jess's teeth grinding as she struggled to bite back her initial retort. Was her desire to minimize this process simply to avoid him after the way her son had taken to him on Saturday? Or because she was as attracted to him as he was to her? Either way, he had no plans to act on that attraction, so she had no reason to worry about spending time with him.

"What department are you with?" he asked.

"Emergency."

Beckett tapped his fingers on the table. That figures, he thought ruefully. "Ambulance services and EMTs fall under your department here, correct?"

"Beckett," his father warned from beside him. Though his voice was low, his dad censored him with only a name. His position had long been clear when it came to Beckett's involvement in anything ambulance related. In fact, it was Beckett's decision to become an EMT in the face of his father's disapproval that had put an additional strain on their already struggling relationship.

Despite how the lack of ambulances and qualified EMTs had taken his favorite child, Beckett's father had never seen a reason to support an expansion of the ambulance program in Woodvale. If anything, Richard Wilder blamed the EMTs for not saving his only daughter.

For Beckett, it had been Sloane's death that steered him toward becoming an EMT. Initially, he had wanted to make sure that no other family suffered such a devastating loss simply because there wasn't a qualified EMT around. But it hadn't taken long before he realized that emergency medicine was his true calling. He'd only accepted the responsibility of these directed donations so that he could finally do what he'd wanted since the night his sister died: get more ambulances and the personnel to staff them up and running in Woodvale. The current service level was the reason his sister was gone. Why was Jess putting up so many objections? They were trying to donate money to improve the medical services available to the town!

As the memories of his sister and the frustration he felt at his father's refusal to accept his chosen career path clouded his brain, he felt emotion well up inside him, and before he could check himself, he snapped, "The emergency department provides a woefully inadequate ambulance service for the town so I would suggest that a one-on-one to secure additional funding would be in your best interests."

CHAPTER FIVE

JESS SHOT TO her feet. Was he accusing her of mismanaging her department? Of...stealing department funds? No way would she take that without argument. And in front of all her peers and colleagues as well. He may have rescued her and Mason from the highway, but calling her work woefully inadequate was more than she could stand.

She slapped her hands down on the table so hard they stung. Who did this egotistical piece of work think he was to come in here and tell them all how to do their jobs?

The youngest son of Richard Wilder, that's who.

She'd learned the hard way that anyone from *that* sort of family couldn't be trusted. And she'd fight tooth and nail to stop another rich man from messing with her head and her life. She wouldn't bow down easily simply because this man's family name hung on one or more walls in this building.

He would not mess with her career. Years of her life had been dedicated to this hospital and building a solid reputation here. Years ago, she'd lost her dignity, her pride and her ability to trust any man in a suit. She'd had to start over when she moved home to Woodvale, but she'd made a name for herself here. She would not lose her hard-earned professional credibility because some jumped-up rich boy thought he knew better than she did how to run her department.

"What exactly are you implying, Mr. Wilder?" The little muscle at the corner of her eye twitched in her fury. Hopefully, it didn't make her appear to be winking neurotically at him. He may look like a Greek god come to life, clad in that custom-tailored suit, but she wouldn't lower herself to flirt with him. If she'd known he was like this she would never have… Never have what? Accepted his help? Let him take her and Mason for ice cream? Reacted to the lightning bolts he set off in her stomach?

Beckett crossed his arms over his chest, and she had to swallow hard at the spark of desire that flared up as the fabric stretched tight over his muscular frame. Not desire, Jess told herself. That's anger, pure and simple. A fact that would be much simpler to remember if he didn't look like God's gift to women. Why couldn't he be homely? Or married? No, he had to be single and drop-dead gorgeous. And Mason hadn't shut up about him since Beckett had dropped them off on Saturday.

He raised one dark eyebrow, and his eyes issued a dare for her to contradict him. "I'm not implying anything, Jess. I just want the best for this hospital and for the town, same as you."

Jess refused to let his arrogant, know-it-all tone make her behave in a way she would regret in front of her colleagues, but she could feel her fury rise up inside her all the same. Before she could do or say something rash, Freya put a calming hand on Jess's arm.

"Okay, you two. I think that's enough for today." Freya flashed them both an icy look.

The chair squeaked and rolled a few inches backward when Jess sat down with an audible harrumph. Having been best friends for five years, Freya had to know how much Beckett's words bothered her. Was she speaking in her role as the assistant hospital administrator or as her friend though? Either way, Jess grudgingly admitted to herself that Freya was right to separate them, and was grateful for the interruption. After all, her department *did* need additional funding and she couldn't afford to risk that by antagonizing the man who would decide how much she got and what she could spend it on. But she didn't have to be happy about it.

Jess kept her gaze focused on Beckett who stared right back at her from across the table. He laced his fingers together on his flat abdomen and leaned back. His pose suggested he was relaxed, but his entire frame held a visible tension. Beckett had an air of dangerousness about him. Like a panther waiting for a moment to strike.

He'd thrown her off-balance from the moment they'd made eye contact. The elder Mr. Wilder had grated on her nerves during the one meeting at which they'd both been in attendance, but Beckett did something far worse—he made her feel things she'd shoved away for years.

Her professionalism served as a shield she wrapped around herself when she entered Woodvale Memorial Hospital. Nothing upset her at work. Personal feelings had no business in the workplace, but today, Beckett had made her forget that. The kindness he'd shown over the weekend and her complicated feelings about that had made it harder for her to remain impartial with him. As a result, his presence had put her on edge and nearly made her lose her temper in a way it would have been hard to come back from with any dignity.

"I think that's the meeting adjourned for today," Mr. Wilder said forcefully. "Make sure you take the information sheet. It has Beckett's contact info on it, and you can set up those individual meetings with him."

Around them, Jess heard and felt the other special committee members filing out of the room. Beckett made no move to leave, so neither did she. The stare-down between them continued. If the only win she could take today was being the last one to blink, so be it.

"Really, guys, you two are ultimately fighting the same war." Freya's voice held a level of exasperation she normally saved for conversations about her on-again, off-again boyfriend. Hearing that tone at work and directed at her made Jess want to wince. "You see that, right? You both want a better-funded emergency department."

"Woodvale needs more staffed ambulances," Beckett said bluntly. "They should be budgeted for."

"I don't disagree with that," Jess allowed. "I just can't fund them out of the current budget from the main hospital emergency department. We're already on a rail-thin margin. You seem to be suggesting that money has been misspent or squandered inefficiently, but every single penny under my control has been accounted for with receipts to prove it and a comprehensive annually reviewed strategy. It's not that I don't want to fund more ambulances—it's that I *do not* have the money to do so without pulling that money away from the nursing staff or the medical supplies."

Beckett closed his eyes. Briefly, resignation crossed his face before he smoothed his features into a more neutral expression. "This is why I want to meet with each department separately. So we can see where the greatest needs are. We want the money to go where it can do the most good."

"And you think the answer is simply to provide another staffed ambulance?" Jess snorted. "We can cart the whole town in here, but if we can't treat them once they get here, how have we done anything good?"

"The two of you need to negotiate a truce." Freya put a hand up to stall any protests. Her face held the serious, no-nonsense expression of a frustrated assistant administrator, but when she walked out of the room, she muttered something under her breath that sounded suspiciously like, "worse than teenagers with a crush."

"Did she just say—? You know what? Never mind." Beckett rolled his shoulders, looking as tense and uncomfortable as Jess felt. "We need to work this out though. She is right about that."

"My responsibility is to make sure that the Emergency Department of this hospital is staffed and stocked with functional equipment. I'm sorry if this frustrates you, but adding more ambulances isn't a high priority for me. It takes funding away from the lifesaving personnel and equipment my department needs to function on a day-to-day basis."

"Ambulances, paramedics and EMTs are the first line of defense when it comes to saving lives," Beckett argued.

Jess could kick herself for walking right into that one. He wasn't wrong. She had all sorts of respect for the first responders who brought the patients in to them each day, and if the budget had any wiggle room at all, she'd gladly agree to the funding increase. The funding just wasn't there. "I know, and I agree, but—"

"There is no but. Ambulances and EMTs are every bit as necessary to your department as X-ray machines and nurses." Beckett's tone was far calmer than earlier, but his impatience still came through loud and clear.

"That may be true, but the budget is still stretched to the point of breaking. Are you going to purchase those ambulances and pay for staff to cover them…forever? What about the supplies to keep them stocked?"

Jess flinched when Beckett suddenly reached

a hand toward her face. She brushed him away before he could touch her. Her fingers grazed his, and even that briefest touch sent her heart rate on a brisk upward climb. "What are you doing?"

"I wasn't going to hurt you, Jess." He hesitated before gesturing at the twitching muscle next to her eye. "Does that happen often?"

"Only when you're around and making wild accusations in front of my colleagues."

Beckett looked like he wanted to say something else, but when he spoke, his tone was neutral. "Would it be possible for me to look at the budget? Maybe I can see ways to finagle it that you haven't. A fresh perspective can often see things overlooked by someone who's been immersed in it, day after day. If that doesn't work, at least we'll have an idea of what direction you should go with your proposal."

Had he phrased it like that earlier, they might not have had such an argument. Her quick temper had flared when he'd called her out like that in a room of her peers. And if he'd hadn't insulted her ability to do her job, then her stupid eye wouldn't be twitching.

Jess couldn't stop the gentle rebuke that formed on her lips. "Asking, rather than accusing…works better every time, you know. I'll need to clear it with Freya for confidentiality reasons but given the current situation I don't see why that would be an issue."

"Can I have your number?"

Heat rushed up over Jess's face. Was he really about to ask her out? After the argument they'd just had? Surely, not.

"That way I can find a good time to look at the data and to follow up regarding the individual meeting."

Of course…

She swallowed hard. As much as she didn't want to date, she wasn't completely immune to the charms of a handsome man. Hopefully, he hadn't caught her moment of girlish stupidity at thinking that he might be flirting with her. Beckett grinned widely when she glanced up at him though.

Great.

The blush would have been bright on her pale face. He wouldn't have missed it. Now he would think she was interested in him. She rattled off her number, stumbling twice over the numerals because she was still so darn shaken.

That's what happens when you barely speak to men, she thought. *You get so out of practice that you don't know what flirting even is!*

When her phone buzzed in her pocket, she nearly jumped out of her skin.

"Now you have mine as well. I promise to

only contact you if it's budget related." Beckett leaned in close, the heat of his breath teasing across her cheek and sending her pulse racing up into an eager pace. The smile he flashed her was nothing short of pure male satisfaction at knowing that a woman was interested in him. "At least until you open the lines of communication to more."

"That will never happen."

"If that's what you want." He shrugged. "You've got my number if you change your mind."

CHAPTER SIX

HE'D THOUGHT HE'D SMOOTHED her ruffled feathers after the initial committee meeting last week, but when he showed up for their scheduled one-on-one discussion, she'd been frostily professional. No, more than that, because most of the time she had looked at him like she might stare at a malfunctioning printer.

But then there had been the rarer moments, when the sparks in Jess's eyes as she looked at him had left Beckett with so many questions. Even though she clearly felt some physical attraction toward him, she remained as prickly as a cactus. She intrigued him. It wasn't just that she didn't fawn over him like most women did. No, this was something more.

Rather than pushing him away though, her standoffish nature made him want to find a chink in her armor. And there were times when he'd catch something fascinating in her expression. She may not like him as a person, yet, but she certainly found something about him impossible to ignore. Occasionally, her eyes glowed with pure female interest and even a hint of longing. And he hadn't missed her reaction when he'd "accidentally" brushed his leg against hers outside the ice cream parlor.

The desire to flirt with her was one he was struggling to squash. He didn't want forever or long-term or any of the things that Jess would be needing. But the drive to win one of her soft smiles was powerful, and when he got one he felt the same rush that he'd experienced in his early days on an ambulance, and he missed that feeling.

"I've seen enough here today, but I'd love to take you to lunch. We could discuss any ideas you have. They don't have to be hospital related." The words came out with the hint of a meaning he hadn't intended, but he figured that a bit of harmless flirtation wouldn't hurt. They both knew the boundaries, after all, and Jess was on the same page as he was. Even if there was an attraction there, she clearly didn't want to give in to it and neither did he. The distance between them was too much to bridge.

Jess shook her head no, just as he'd known she would. "I don't think that would be a good idea."

"No?" He took a step closer. When her hair

dipped down into her face, he gave in to the urge and swept it back before tucking it behind her ear. That wasn't an outright no, and something about the shy look that the normally confident woman was giving him tempted him. "How about dinner then?"

"You wish, Captain Trust Fund." Pink tinted her cheeks, the blush coloring her soft skin and making her even more beautiful, but the defenses in her eyes backed up her words. Jess didn't just have walls—she had a moat filled with alligators.

He'd picked up that stupid nickname around the hospital once it came out that he'd been an EMT captain before he came back to Woodvale and was from *the* Wilder family. He didn't love the assumptions behind the label, but it had never really bothered him much until he heard it roll off Jess's lips. She'd probably be surprised to learn that while he did technically have a trust fund, he couldn't access it for a few more years. After the way his sister had blown through money—including well into the six figures for a sports car that she let her fiancé drive far too fast and which had ultimately led to their deaths—Richard Wilder had locked Beckett's own trust fund up tight.

Beckett had worked for a living, something Sloane had never had to do. In fact, he missed being just plain old Captain Beckett Wilder, EMT. He'd hung up the uniform and traded it for custom tailored suits when his dad's cancer diagnosis had come in, reluctantly accepting the mantle of being Richard Wilder's heir and next in command on an official level. He hadn't realized the toll not being on an action-filled ambulance would take on his soul though. Man, he missed the adrenaline rush that came when that bell went off. Thankfully, it was just temporary. He couldn't wait to get back to his real career.

Leaning a little closer, Beckett dropped his voice and teased Jess a bit. "What if I up the ante to dinner and breakfast the next morning? Could you get a sitter for Mason for Saturday night?"

"You are incorrigible. I've got to get to work," she muttered and walked away without a backward glance.

"That wasn't a no," he called after her.

The tiniest hint of a laugh just reached his ears. His lips twitched at the sound. One day soon he'd get a full laugh from her. He'd make sure of it.

"Beckett," Freya said, pulling his attention away from Jess's retreating form.

"Hmm…?" When Jess scanned her ID badge and went through the doors that led back into the emergency department, Beckett turned to

Freya who stared at him with this stern teacher face. "What?"

"Don't toy with her." She crossed her arms and rose up on tiptoe so that she could properly look him in the eye. "Don't start anything that you aren't serious about."

"Wasn't planning on it," Beckett reassured her. Freya was a good friend, and she was only looking out for Jess's best interests. "Jess and I are on the same page. She's completely safe with me, so don't worry."

Freya gave him a skeptical look but let the subject drop. "Don't you have a meeting to get to?"

"I met with Jess this morning. I was supposed to meet with General Surgery, but they had an emergency surgery pop up so had to reschedule."

He and Jess had gone over the numbers, but he'd had to admit that she was right. The budget as it was just wouldn't allow for more ambulances. It wouldn't even cover the empty EMT position that had been sitting open for months. Hammering on about ambulances wasn't going to get it done though. No, this issue would have to come from higher up the food chain because more funding would have to be allocated from above. He'd asked Jess to submit the proposal to include ambulances, salaries and supplies on top of the things she'd pointed out this morning, like a replacement for their ancient X-ray machine, though this was more than the scope of what could be covered by a one-time donation.

"Ah, well, I take it things didn't go your way?"

Frowning, he asked, "What makes you say that?"

She pointed at his face. "Those crinkles of frustration around your eyes. They make you look like your father."

Taking a deep breath, Beckett tried to relax his face. One day he would look like his father, but he wasn't quite ready for that yet. "I'm trying to get more ambulances and EMTs so that what happened with Sloane doesn't happen again. Jess and I spent all morning looking at the numbers though and she's right. There is no wiggle room. The hospital needs to do a better job funding that department."

"You know how those bean counters are. If it doesn't affect their bottom line, they're gonna kick that can down the road as far as they can." Freya shrugged; she'd been fighting against the system for years and knew there was no easy fix. She started walking away, but tossed over her shoulder, "If you want to beat the rain, you might want to hurry."

Beckett wanted to hit the gym and work off

some of the frustrations seeing that budget had brought up. *And the tension from being so close to Jess in that tiny closet-sized office.* Exercise usually helped give him clarity and he needed it to find a way to get the services he wanted funded. *And put the soft scent of Jess's light perfume out of his mind.* The pitch-black sky made him second-guess that choice. The cars in the lot were nearly impossible to see through the furious rain. A large piece of something yellow flew past the window and stuck to one of the columns marking the pedestrian crossing, flapping like a canary's wings against its constraint. Staying at the hospital a while longer seemed like a better plan.

His phone buzzed, and when he pulled it out of his pocket, an emergency notice flashed across the screen. The weather alert he read on the screen sent a shiver down his spine. This was not good.

"Everyone move to an interior hallway!" He jumped into action and shepherded people away from the wall of glass at the front of the hospital, urging them farther into the building. "There's a tornado just outside Woodvale and it's heading our way."

CHAPTER SEVEN

THE ENTIRE EMERGENCY DEPARTMENT fell into chaos. Panicking patients shoved stressed employees as they tried to get deeper into the building. Doctors and nurses steered others through the hallways to a safer part of the hospital. Jess got caught up ensuring patient safety. Thankfully, her meeting with Beckett had ended, so she could devote her time to helping the overwhelmed emergency room staff.

Jess groaned when, instead of moving with the others to safety, one of their medical receptionists crawled under her desk. Apparently, Sasha's flight-or-fight mode had triggered the third option of freeze. Jess would worry about getting her out once she'd gotten everyone else sorted. She had to focus on the people she could help right now.

"You'd think they'd never lived through a storm before," Jess muttered to herself. With a disbelieving shake of her head, Jess helped a patient into a wheelchair. After pushing her to the designated hallway, Jess left her with one of the nurse's assistants.

The squeak, squeak, squeak of Jess's shoes kept her company as she hurried back to the ED. The few stragglers were heading in the right direction. One man limped along holding on to a friend, slowly trekking up the hallway.

After grabbing another wheelchair, Jess jogged their direction with it. "Here, this will make the trip go a lot faster."

She took one last look around the department. All clear. With a glance up to the ceiling, Jess sent up a quick prayer that the damage to the hospital would be minimal, and the elementary school wouldn't be in the tornado's path. *And above all else, please keep Mason safe.* As soon as she got herself to safety, she was going to pull up that weather app and see if there was a projected path. She'd taken three steps toward that interior hallway when the sound of crying hit her ears and she remembered.

Sasha...

Only the terrified medical receptionist remained, still sobbing beneath her desk. The poor girl was frozen with fright, but with the large bank of windows right above the desk it would not be safe for her to stay. How could Jess get Sasha to go with her though?

"Sasha, we need to get to the hallway, come on." Keeping her voice low and steady, Jess tried to reason with the woman even though her own heart raced like a Thoroughbred at Keeneland racetrack. "I don't think this is a good place to stay. We need to move away from these windows."

Outside those windows, the sky held nearly no light. A roar grew louder and louder. Jess swallowed hard. This was so not good. Why did there have to be a tornado on her watch? She didn't have time for this today.

"Please, Sasha, let's go!" Jess crouched down and held out a hand. Calm and collected wasn't working with the medical receptionist. Maybe authoritative? It might work if the panicked woman didn't notice how bad Jess's hand was shaking. "Sasha, get out of there now!"

Sasha rocked back and forth, eyes wild with fear. She ignored Jess's outstretched hand. The orders Jess had issued fell on effectively deaf ears. Between sobs, Sasha muttered a prayer.

"The good Lord helps those who help themselves." Jess sighed. "And Sasha, you really gotta help yourself right now."

"She's not coming out," a man's voice called from right above Jess's head. "Leave her."

Jess jerked, slamming her head into the edge of Sasha's desk. Pain rocketed through her skull, radiating out from the point of impact. No good deed goes unpunished. Hadn't life taught her that by now?

"Sorry to startle you." Beckett held out a hand. "You aren't safe here. Come on."

Jess put her hand in his and let him pull her to her feet. As she rose to her full unimpressive height, she got a good look outside the window. No longer inky black, the sky now held an odd tint. Through the murky green glow, she could just make out the funnel cloud.

"Oh!"

Beckett must have seen it just as Jess did. He shoved her under another desk, blocking the opening with his body. His voice lowered to a growl. "Get down."

Something large and heavy crashed through the glass and hit the floor nearby. Jess's view, however, consisted solely of Beckett's broad chest. The wind blew his tie, whipping the silk up around her face. She brushed it down and held it to his chest. Tension locked his frame into a protective barrier. He took the brunt of the wind and rain, sheltering her, protecting her from the onslaught.

Metallic pings rang out sharply and contrasted with the roar of the wind. Objects hitting the tile floors created an erratic tempo. Beckett grunted as his back was pelted, the muffled thumps adding to the din surrounding them.

"Is that hail?" They were inches apart, but the deafening roar of the wind nearly drowned out Jess's words.

"Not sure if it's hail or what," he yelled back. "Stings though."

The desk Beckett had shoved Jess under started sliding back as the floor grew wet. Beckett crept along, keeping as much of the protection of the desk as he could. Still, the wind continued.

Water puddled up under her, and her scrubs soaked up the icy liquid like a wick.

The wind stopped, suddenly, as if someone had flipped a switch and the room grew quiet. "Is it over?"

Beckett groaned and eased back from the desk. "I think it might be."

"Oh, man." Jess crawled out and stumbled to her feet. "That was terrifying."

Jess couldn't identify the impulse that overtook her logic. Relief at being alive? Gratitude for his protection? It could have been any number of reasons, but before she could second-guess it, she flung herself against Beckett's chest. Instinct drove her. Wrapping her arms around his neck, she tugged his face down. Her lips were nearly to his before the dots connected in her brain that she was standing on her tiptoes, about to kiss Beckett Wilder.

Stress. It had to be stress. Or maybe pure appreciation that she was alive and safe thanks to him. There could be no other rationale for why she'd have nearly made a mistake that monumental. Releasing him as quickly as she grabbed him, Jess stuttered over an apology.

"It's okay," he said slowly, but there was a hint of something in his eyes. Something vibrant, eager and far too intriguing.

"I'm sorry," she murmured. "Adrenaline got me."

New subject required. Right now, before she stupidly threw herself at him again. She needed to do a status check. Physically, she was in great shape. Wet, but uninjured. Mentally, she was shaken.

This area of the hospital hadn't fared quite so well. The emergency department looked like a war zone. Spinning in a slow circle, she tried to take it all in. Broken glass was scattered across the floor, glittering in the odd light. Dripping-wet sections of insulation hung from the ceiling like sad party streamers. Papers and brochures littered the floor and flat surfaces. Computer monitors were upended. The emergency lights flickered as if the generator couldn't decide if it was needed or not. Everything around them was either broken, soaked or both.

"Are you okay?" Beckett's color looked a little off. But, then again, they had just survived a tornado.

"I am thanks to you." Jess probably didn't look her best either, even though he'd protected her from the worst of it. "Do you know what the expected path was for the tornado? Was it heading for the elementary school?"

"I have no idea," he said, leaning against one of the supports. Blood appeared at his shoulder and trickled down the white column. "My back doesn't feel so great."

She strode over to him. "Take off that jacket."

"I kinda like it when you're bossy." He winced as the suit coat slid from his shoulders.

She took the jacket from him. There were dozens of holes in it. "Okay, shirt off too. Let me see your back."

"If you wanted to see me without a shirt, all you had to do was ask." He tried for a grin, but it was weak. Once crisp, the white button-down was now ragged. He tugged it gently from his torso. A grimace marred his handsome face when the shirt stuck to a cut on his shoulder. "This went on a lot easier than it's coming off."

Blood speckled the back of the shirt. He turned his back to her, and Jess had to bite her lip to avoid a gasp. Dozens of little shards of metal were embedded into his skin.

"I need to find some supplies. Don't lean against anything else until I get all that shrapnel out." If Beckett hadn't pushed her under that desk, those metal slivers could have been lodged in her face. She let out a long sigh. She didn't like the wave of concern that washed over her. It's gratitude, she told herself. Just gratitude. Taking a deep breath to regain her focus, Jess began looking for the supplies she'd need to remove the debris from his back.

"Do you think you could try to find out what else got hit in town?" she asked as she searched through a tipped-over supply cart for an undamaged package of gauze. "Start with the elementary school, please. I need to see if Mason is okay."

"I'll see what I can find out," Beckett called as she rifled through the remains of a storage cart. "Look out for that ceiling though. It looks like it could fall at any time."

Jess gave a quick glance up. One ceiling tile hung precariously above her head. Why wasn't this place constructed of sturdier materials? Probably so that rich men like Beckett and Clint could have more money to spend on asinine things like fancy cars and golf tee times. She stopped herself; that was a mean thought about the man who had probably just saved her life. What was wrong with her?

Where were the dang tweezers? Finally, she found a pair.

"Watch out!" Beckett's strong arms pulled her into his bare chest and away from the sudden crash of falling debris. Jess's heart raced. Was it because a giant chunk of ceiling had nearly flattened her into a scrub-covered pancake or because she was being pressed into the deliciously muscled chest of a good-looking man who'd saved her life twice now in the span of an hour?

The ceiling, Jess. It has to be the ceiling because you cannot start liking any part of Beckett. Not even a chest so perfectly sculpted as his. Didn't you learn your lesson about messing with a rich guy?

"Thank you," she muttered as she pushed away from his chest. Images flashed through her mind of having her hands on his body during a more intimate encounter. Swallowing hard, Jess pulled herself together. She was a professional, not some lovelorn woman who couldn't control herself around a handsome man. "You're going to make your back worse if you don't stay still."

"Are you really gonna stand there and chastise me? Woman, I just saved you. Where's my gratitude?" He shook his head.

"Once everything is clear, I'll set up a parade. We can start right here at the hospital and parade down Main Street."

Main Street... Oh, my goodness, what else has been hit? My house? The elementary school? Mason!

Where was her phone? Jess patted her pockets, searching for the missing device. Nothing. Quickly, she scanned the room. She'd clad her phone in a hot-pink case. How hard could it be to find? She grabbed one of the desk phones. No dial tone.

Of course.

"Do you have a phone?" She held her hand out impatiently.

He reached for his discarded suit coat. From the inner pocket, he pulled a cell phone. "Who do you need to call?"

"I want to check on the elementary school."

"Of course. I was about to do that when I realized that ceiling was going to drop on your head." He held out his phone, and Jess took it from his outstretched hand.

What was the number? Her hands shook so badly that she nearly dropped the phone. Why couldn't she remember the number for the elementary school? This was the downfall of programming numbers into phones and no longer having to dial them. No one, including Jess, memorized numbers anymore.

"Can't remember the number?"

She clutched the phone close in case he had ideas of taking it back. "I just need a moment."

Typing in the area code, she hoped that the familiarity of those numbers on the screen would help trigger the memory of the rest. Thankfully, it worked. She typed in the rest and hit Dial.

Instead of an answer, or even the sound of the call ringing through, she was met with an automated voice saying that the call could not be completed at this time and to please try again later.

"Won't go through." The lump clogging her throat made her sound like a croaking frog.

"Probably too many people trying to make calls, either for help or to check on their loved ones."

"You think?"

"Lines and towers may be down. Or are simply overloaded." He gently took the phone back. "Let me see if I can make a call." He tapped on his screen and then held the phone up to his ear. "It won't even call one of my preprogrammed contacts. I think cells are just down."

"Landlines too." Jess nodded toward the dead phone on the desk. "At least that one is, anyway. If the tornado hit the school, there could be a lot of injured kids. We need to make contact and see if they need help."

He nodded. "Okay. Get this shrapnel out of my back and I'll find a way to make contact. Even if I have to drive over there myself."

CHAPTER EIGHT

"Beckett—"

"I'll see if I can get a text or call out while you get this mess out of me." When Jess didn't move, Beckett gave a little more encouragement that he hoped would appeal to her nursing background. "You don't want to be responsible for my back getting infected after I saved your life, do you?"

Crossing her arms over her chest, Jess snapped, "You're never going to let me forget that, are you?"

"Nope." Turning, he grinned at her over his shoulder, happy that his tactics seemed to be working. He was learning how her mind worked and guessed correctly when he'd narrowed in on her professional sensibilities. She'd never leave someone to get an infection she could help prevent, especially not someone who had helped her. He did feel the slightest smidgen of guilt himself that he had to use that against her, but he needed her to focus. And he needed the metal slivers out of his back, for sure. "But think of how much you'll enjoy the pain of pulling these bits out. You can really enjoy torturing me."

Jess grew quiet, but she gathered the rest of the supplies needed to pick his back clean. He knew she was worried about her son. He had to admit, he was worried about the little guy too. There was something about that kid that Beckett found hard to forget.

Kinda like his mama.

Unlike Mason, Jess didn't want to talk. She was probably only speaking to him in that moment because he'd forced the issue. By being in the right place at the right time to save her life, or at least her pretty face, from the shrapnel she was about to extract from his back with tweezers, he'd earned at least a scrap of respect from her. Maybe that would push them over the line from enemies to friends on which they'd teetered recently. A few times, he'd noticed a softening in her demeanor, so quick he nearly missed it, but if he opened his mouth, she slammed those defenses into place so fast it nearly gave him whiplash.

Occasionally, her hands on his back softened into more of a caress than a strictly professional touch though. Her spur-of-the-moment almost-kiss sat front and center in Beckett's mind. Had it been a by-product of adrenaline or something more? The look in her eyes had been far more than gratitude. He'd adamantly refused to consider anything more than a friendly professional relationship with her, albeit one with a little good-natured flirting, but the way it felt to have her pressed against his chest tempted him to reconsider.

Teeth grinding together, Beckett bit back a curse. She'd dug way in to get that piece out. He'd teased her about torture, but maybe she'd taken that as an order. Geez, that hurt. He puffed out a breath, trying to breathe through the pain. The only good thing about it was that it distracted him from his increasingly intimate thoughts of Jess. He needed to remember that he wasn't interested in long-term, and Jess practically had the word *forever* stamped across her pretty face.

"I think that's the last of it. That piece was in the deepest." She moved around him to make eye contact, but she seemed to have trouble meeting his eyes, with her gaze focusing more on his chest than his face. "I still need to bandage you up. I hate to put a dozen small bandages on your back, so what do you think of one larger piece of gauze?"

"Both sound annoying. Do what you think is best." He trusted her medical judgment.

When she'd finished with the bandage and removed her gloves, tossing them into a trash can that she'd righted, air whooshed from Beckett's lungs and he breathed a deep sigh of relief. He had needed her ever-so-enticing hands off his bare skin. The more Jess touched him, the more his thoughts drifted to places they shouldn't.

Picking up his discarded dress shirt, Beckett's nose wrinkled. The blood stains would never come out, not to mention the multiple poke holes. Easing one arm through the sleeve, his lip curled up in disgust when the crusty, dried blood scraped against his skin. How inappropriate would it be for him to be roaming the halls of the hospital half-dressed?

"Don't put that nasty thing back on." Jess tossed something blue his direction. "That scrub top will look silly with those fancy pants of yours, but at least it's clean."

"My pants aren't fancy." Looking down, Beckett frowned. They were tailored, yes, but they were a classic-cut suit pant. Hardly fancy.

"That suit probably cost more than my car," she said dryly.

He didn't let the retort fly that her car wasn't worth much. His gut feeling said it wouldn't go over well. The car might be a broken-down hunk of junk, but it was hers, and he'd learned already that she was protective of what was hers.

"And now it's trash." Beckett shrugged, refusing to wince at the pain that little gesture caused. "There are…certain expectations that come with being a Wilder. Expensive suits are one of them."

Expensive suits, five-star restaurants, and oversize houses on the lake. None of it was really who Beckett was, though it came part and parcel of carrying the Wilder name. They hadn't managed to pry the keys to his truck from his hands just yet, but he worried the day was coming when his dad forced a luxury car on him with the admonishment of "What will people think if they see you stepping out of a pickup truck? Beckett, you are a Wilder, but we are not wild."

Jess tossed a reply over her shoulder as she walked away. "Imagine the ambulances you could fund without all the posh trappings that you seem to hate anyways."

Beckett gingerly slipped the blue scrub top over his head. It really seemed to irk her that his family had money. What he didn't know was why. If she'd take even a minute to get to know him, she'd see he wasn't the guy she imagined him to be.

When he caught up, she was trying to clear some debris blocking the hallway into the main hospital; that explained why none of the other hospital staff or patients had appeared yet. He took a chunk of busted ceiling tile from her hands and threw it down the hallway. It shattered against the wall. Side by side, they silently dislodged debris so they could access the hospital. Every movement made him aware of all the small cuts on his back, but it had to be done. Was there more devastation on the other side or had the emergency department sustained the brunt of it?

Soon, they cleared the doorway. As soon as they opened it, Freya appeared. She looked frazzled, but nearly as immaculate as when they'd spoken earlier. Peeking beyond her into the hospital, Beckett could see some broken glass and overturned chairs, but nothing too bad.

"Jess!" Freya cried as she ran into Jess's outstretched arms. "Oh, thank goodness. I couldn't find you and I thought…"

Beckett watched the two women embrace with no small amount of envy.

"I'm good. I don't have a scratch on me." Jess looked Beckett's way and her lips tipped up in the briefest hint of a smile. "Someone took the brunt for me. How are you?"

Freya took Jess's hands in hers and the expression on her face gave Beckett pause. She seemed to be steeling her nerves before she could share her news. Dread dropped in the pit of his stomach. It sat heavy and solid, stirring up his adrenaline again. Nothing she was about to say could be good.

"Jess, we got a radio call. Woodvale Elementary was directly in the tornado's path. There's no word on how bad it is yet, but part of the building has collapsed."

"Freya..." Jess breathed more than she said.

Her knees gave way, and she would have hit the ground if Beckett hadn't moved to catch her. She shook against him. Mason was her everything, if something had happened to him, Beckett wasn't sure how she'd handle that.

The sudden action sent little stabs of pain across the entirety of his back as the cuts were pulled and scrunched, but he seemed to be programmed to protect Jess. Even at his own peril.

"I have to go there." Jess's voice cracked, sounding nothing like her normally smooth tones.

"You have to pull yourself together and be strong." Freya pulled Jess in for another hug. She held on for a moment, holding so tight that it looked like she was trying to lend Jess her strength. "Okay, so, listen to me. The plan is for us to send someone over to set up a first-aid tent. I'm getting some supplies together and need to find someone who we can spare to go when we are already going to be strapped here."

"I'll go," Jess volunteered.

"Honey, I don't think it's a good idea. You're not in the right mindset to treat patients." Freya looked apologetic, but Beckett could see that denying Jess was costing his old friend. "We are trying to rouse one of the off-duty EMTs, but phones are down everywhere."

"I'll go." They didn't need to get in touch with another EMT. He was standing right there and more than willing to help. "I'm available and I have the experience. You don't need to short the hospital when I'm happy to step up."

Freya nodded. "Yes. This is good. Thank you, Beckett."

"I need to go to that school," Jess argued, crossing her arms over her chest. The defiant look on her face said she was going with or without permission. "I'm okay. I can handle this."

She did seem steadier on her feet than a moment ago, but a certain fragility surrounded her. Maybe because he'd already protected her several times that day, or maybe because of the way his heart had skipped a beat when she'd nearly kissed him, he didn't want to see her upset any more. "I am qualified to do this. Just because

I've spent more time recently in suits than in the back of an ambo doesn't mean I've forgotten my training. And no one here is counting on my presence. We don't know how many kids are injured. Do you honestly believe that you can maintain enough emotional detachment to treat the others if Mason is injured?"

Terror flashed in her eyes, stronger now than when they were under that desk. Her eyes closed for a moment, lashes fanning across her cheeks, and when they opened, determination replaced the fear. "I'm going to find my son, with or without you. Now, if you will excuse me, I don't have time to argue with you."

CHAPTER NINE

THOUGHTS OF WHAT could be happening at the school rushed through Jess's head, like scenes from the most traumatic movie ever made. Her brain quite vividly showed her images of injured children, maimed teachers, and worst of all, the numerous ways that her own son could have been harmed.

My sweet boy...

She pictured him with glass in his little body, like she'd just pulled from Beckett's back, with broken bones, and—she swallowed hard—worse... She blinked away the tears that final image brought forth. Breathing grew hard. *Don't panic yet, Jess.* He could be fine. Mason could be perfectly fine. But the growing lump in the pit of her stomach wasn't going away until she could verify with her own eyes that her little boy was healthy and whole.

"Do you really think this is the best course of action?" Beckett asked from behind her.

Jess spun to face him. Why was he still here? His presence at the moment served as a distraction she didn't want or need, and he should have been heading over to the school since he had volunteered to do so. "I really will be okay."

She had no choice. Panicking was a luxury that she didn't have. Most people might not think of being able to panic as a luxury, but when you were a single mom, there was no one else to lean on. She'd had her moment of freakout, but now she had to focus. With her job, she compartmentalized things every day, removing emotions from the equation. It was harder to do with her own son potentially in danger, but now she had to.

"I know you are worried about Mason, but it's that fear that might make you make a mistake today. You need to trust me."

"Trust you…"

Once upon a time, she'd been an eternal optimist who would put her faith in anyone and everyone. When she was a young, idealistic nursing student, she still thought men could be trusted and naively believed in all the other romantic jazz—love at first sight, soul mates and even the idea that she could find the man of her dreams. When she'd met Clint, she thought she'd found her forever. He'd swept her off her feet so hard that she doubted her feet touched the ground that entire summer.

It had been perfect.

Until she found out it was all a lie.

It was crushing to find out that her entire world was based on falsehoods and secrets, but she got through it. And if it made her more wary of men like Beckett, she was better for it. Men couldn't be trusted, particularly ones with more zeros at the end of their bank balances than limbs on their body.

One amazing thing did come from that relationship with Clint—Mason.

Right now, Mason might be in trouble. And she wasn't going to let anyone keep her from her son any longer. But she wasn't about to lower her guard and trust Beckett or any other man.

"Fine, let's go." She headed for the main supply closet. She wanted to get those supplies and get to the school. She left Beckett to trail behind her. She made it ten feet before she stopped cold in her tracks, realizing that she'd left someone else behind—Sasha.

Sprinting back through the ED, she looked for the other woman. "Sasha? Are you here, honey? Call out if you can hear me."

"Is that the woman under the desk?" Beckett asked. He was tenacious; she'd give him that.

"Yeah, she's one of our medical receptionists." Jess looked under each desk as she passed it. So far, she could see no sign of the frightened young woman. Where could she be?

"There," Beckett said, pointing to where a single white sneaker and scrub-clad leg poked out of a pile of debris. "Help me uncover her."

Working swiftly, but carefully, they started to uncover Sasha. "Do you think there's enough weight on her that we need to worry about crush syndrome?" Jess asked. While she was confident in her nursing abilities, she had never worked Search and Rescue or as an EMT. She saw the injuries after the patient had reached the hospital and at the very least some lifesaving measures had already been applied.

Beckett moved more debris. "I think if we move quickly, she won't have been under the weight for long enough for that to be a factor. It hasn't been fifteen minutes yet, so we should be okay to completely uncover her. We could be dealing with some crush injuries though, for sure."

Jess checked Sasha's foot. "No pulse."

Beckett moved enough to find Sasha's other foot where he too sought for a pulse. With a negative shake of his head, he said, "Nothing here either."

Quickly, they cleared the rest of the debris from Sasha's body. Her chest and head had been partially protected, thankfully, by an overturned office chair. Once they had her fully uncovered, Jess started checking vitals.

"Pulse is weak. Not seeing any respirations." She scrubbed her fingers against Sasha's sternum. "Sasha, honey, can you hear me?"

The medical receptionist didn't respond to the stimuli that Jess provided. *Dang it.* Jess pressed her palm against Sasha's forehead and lifted her chin to make sure her airway was open. She leaned forward, hoping to feel the woman's breath against her face. Nothing. "She's not breathing."

"Starting CPR." Beckett moved into position next to Sasha's shoulders and placed the heel of his palm on the center of Sasha's chest. He counted out the chest compressions.

When that was done, she gave the required breaths. She looked around for a mask or Ambu Bag, but none were visible.

Beckett continued chest compressions until Sasha started to cough and pushed him away.

"Wh-what happened?" she asked, trying to lift her head.

"Hey, take it easy. Lie back down for me." Beckett put a gentle hand on her shoulder. "A tornado hit the hospital and you were knocked unconscious. Don't try to move just yet. It would be best if we could get you checked out properly before you move too much."

Sasha blinked rapidly, her eyes struggling to focus. "My head hurts."

Jess was certain that the younger woman had a concussion. The worry was that she had far more than a concussion—internal injuries or something. A lot of very hard materials, some with fairly substantial weight, had fallen on Sasha.

"Yeah, I'd imagine it does. Hold still." Beckett kept his hand on her shoulder, preventing her from moving much. "Jess, you think you could go find some help? I'll stay with Sasha and make sure that she doesn't move much until we get her good and checked out."

Jess hesitated to go, preferring to stay with Sasha herself, but Beckett had the woman calm and Sasha was responding well to his relaxed demeanor. So she rose to her feet. "I'll be back as quickly as I can."

She hurried to the main lobby where Freya had said they were setting up a temporary ED. "We have an injured medical receptionist back in the ED. I need a doctor and a gurney. I'm not sure if it's safe to move her. We did have to perform CPR, but she's conscious now and talking."

Within a minute, Jess had a doctor and a

nurse following her back to where Sasha and Beckett were. Beckett still sat on his knees next to Sasha making sure she stayed as still and calm as possible.

"Hey, Jess," Freya called. "Tina has all those supplies together. If Beckett is ready, you can hand off your patient to Dr. Newton and get on over to the school now. Be careful and check in when you can, okay?"

CHAPTER TEN

"I'LL GET MY CAR." Jess took off out the door, leaving Beckett no choice but to follow her. Now that they'd handed Sasha off to the care of one of the emergency department doctors, she was gung ho about getting to the school. He went out the door a few paces behind her, but he had to pause because he couldn't see. He blinked several times at the sudden difference in light. Man, it was bright out there.

When his eyes adjusted, he saw Jess standing a few feet away, staring, hand up over her mouth. He figured she'd be halfway to her car by now. Maybe the change in light had gotten to her too.

"What's wrong…?" But then he took in all the devastation outside, and words failed him. Even after seeing the havoc inside the emergency department, the scene outside managed to shock him.

Trees and power poles were down all around

the hospital. In the parking lot, several cars were completely flipped upside down. Several more had been tipped onto their sides. Many of the vehicles had no glass left in them.

They walked carefully through the debris-laden lot. Not a single vehicle seemed to have been spared. Even the ones that remained on all four tires were covered in tree branches, or pieces of trash.

"Well, I guess we aren't taking my car." Jess stopped in front of her aged black sedan and let out a shaky breath. "I just picked it up from the shop too!"

The car had another vehicle tipped into the side of it, and the little black sedan was partially crushed under the load that the much larger SUV put on it. There was no way they were getting that car out alone. Even if they could have freed it, the car's road worthiness remained questionable.

"Okay, well, let's take my truck then," Beckett said, steering Jess toward the parking garage with a gentle hand on her elbow. It had only been a few hours since he'd made the drive to the hospital, but it seemed like it had been days. Time had a way of becoming uncertain when traumatic things happened. He knew that, but the reminder still slapped him in the face hard.

They hadn't made it one hundred yards before they saw the live power line down across the exit of the parking garage. The wind blew a branch in and out of contact with it. Blue sparks of electricity shot up at every contact. He let out a low curse.

"So, it looks like yours isn't an option either. What now?" Jess closed her eyes and looked up to the sky. Was she praying? Beckett realized that he had no idea if she was religious or spiritual in any way.

"The school is only about eight blocks that way." She opened her eyes and pointed north. "We could walk. We'd have to take even fewer supplies though. You might be as strong as an ox, but I don't think you could cart all that for long, especially with your back the way it is."

"At least it looks like the rain is gone." Beckett tried to recognize the one positive he'd found since they'd walked outside. He wasn't looking forward to walking eight blocks in wet dress shoes though. The blisters he'd get from that would be the size of dinner plates. He had his gym bag in the truck, and if he was lucky, his sneakers were with it.

He took a deep breath and stared at the parking garage. Woodvale Memorial's parking structure was multilevel, but the drive lanes were far too narrow to have two vehicles pass and not hit the parked cars. Very much a one-way only. An idea sparked, but the only way it would work was if Jess didn't let anyone else come in. "I can possibly get my truck out if I drive down the entrance. If you can block any other cars from driving into the garage, I'll give it a try."

She nodded. Once again, she took off walking without a word, leaving Beckett to scramble to keep pace. For someone so tiny, she sure could move when she wanted to.

"Have you always lived in Woodvale?" he asked as he caught up with her.

She shot him a look. "What?"

He hoped his random attempts at conversation would help keep her mind off the situation at the elementary school and her terror of not knowing what was happening with her son. He shrugged in response to her question. "It looks like we're going to be spending a lot of time together today. Maybe we could talk a little— unless you'd rather spend it in awkward silence, that is."

"Yes."

"Yes, you've always lived in Woodvale, or yes, you'd rather go all day without speaking?"

"Both, really."

Becket chuckled. "I'm not great at silence. Never have been. So, you might as well accept that I'm just going to talk even if you don't participate much in the conversation."

"Oh, joy."

"I grew up here too. Not sure how I didn't know you before?"

"I don't get out much."

Her deadpan delivery made him snort. "For your entire life?"

They walked around the parking garage to the entrance and Beckett noticed that the streetlights on the corner weren't functioning.

"Go get your truck, or I'll hoof it with all the supplies I can carry alone."

"Got it." He left her standing in the entrance of the garage and hurried to where he'd parked his truck.

The parking garage seemed to have withstood the storm without much damage. He saw a few busted windows, likely from the debris thrown by that wicked wind, but most of the vehicles in the garage appeared to be in drivable condition. Thankfully, his truck was intact.

He drove carefully back down the entrance ramp. To get out, you normally had to circle through all the levels to the top, then circle back down the other side. He really hoped that Jess was blocking anyone else from coming into the garage, because it was too tight for even a small car to pass by his truck.

When he could finally see daylight again, he could also see Jess. She stood in front of the entrance, squaring off with a guy in an SUV try-ing to turn into the garage. He backed down when he saw Beckett's truck.

Jess ran over and hopped into the passenger seat. "Took you long enough," she muttered. "I nearly got murdered while you were in here ca-ressing your leather seats."

Snorting, Beckett didn't give her any further reply. Fear already had her in a snit, and he wasn't going to push her into taking more of that frustration out on him. He pulled around the front of the hospital, getting as close as he could to the emergency department given the downed trees and flipped vehicles.

"Let's get the supplies and go." She jumped out before he'd even put the truck in Park.

"That was the plan," he muttered under his breath. This was going to be a long day if she insisted on flying solo for everything yet being angry with him for not keeping up.

He followed her inside where a pile of sup-plies had been set aside for them to take. "Any-thing else you think we will need?" he asked as he sorted through some of it. It would be easier to grab anything else they needed while they were still here, rather than having to come back because they had overlooked something necessary.

"It's not a fully loaded trauma room or even

a stocked ambulance, but hopefully it will be enough for first aid for the elementary school. There's a huge stock of bandages, gauze, antiseptic, a portable defibrillator that I'm praying we don't need, plus KT tape and wrap for any sprains."

"Instant cold packs? Gloves?"

"Yup." Jess stood, hefting up one of the large bins. She nodded her head toward the two remaining bins of supplies. "Can you get those?"

Freya motioned to Beckett to join her for a moment. When he walked over, she lowered her voice. "I need you to look out for her today. Especially if…" Her words trailed off but Beckett knew exactly what the rest of that sentence would have contained.

Especially if something had happened to Mason…

"I promise you I'll not let her out of my sight."

"Thank you." Freya reached out and put a hand on his arm. "But you'd better go, because she's leaving without you."

He turned to see Jess walking out the doors with her arms loaded down. Beckett hoisted the rest of the supplies and followed her once more. She was waiting next to the truck. Pressing his load against the side of the truck, Beckett fished his keys out of his pocket and unlocked the back doors. Soon, all the supplies were in the backseat. He dug quickly through his gym bag and changed his dress shoes for dry socks and sneakers.

Jess huffed a protest, but thankfully didn't say anything. This was a fight he wasn't going to engage in though. He needed dry shoes, or he'd have blisters and need medical treatment himself. Simple as that. Tossing the wet shoes in the back, he slid behind the wheel.

He turned north out of the parking lot. With all the debris on the roads, he had to creep along, well below the speed limit. From the impatient noises coming from the passenger seat, he sensed the pace was killing Jess. Couldn't be helped though since he had to weave and dodge around downed trees and wrecked cars. It wasn't safe to drive anywhere close to the posted speed limit. They'd be of no use to anyone if they crashed before they made it to the school.

When he made the turn off Main onto Wood Street, the most direct route to the school, that's when things got really jammed up. There were several large tree branches in the street, blocking both drive lanes. Beckett hit the brakes and brought the truck to a quick stop.

"Can we move them?" Jess asked.

"We can look and see." He put the truck in

Park and stepped out. As he moved up to get a better look, he could see that the road was completely impassable. Even in a truck, trying to go over limbs that size would be dangerous, and they'd take too much time to move.

"This is going to be a no-go. We're better off going back to Main."

"Shh…" Jess held up one finger—*wait*.

"What are you—?" The rest of his words were muffled by her hand covering his mouth.

"I said, shh. Could you please be quiet?" She whispered her words as she stood against his chest, her palm pressed to his lips. "I heard something."

Blood raced through his veins, and he couldn't have heard anything over the pounding of his pulse. His body was all too aware of how close she was and how much closer they could get. His hands came up to rest on her waist.

His grip tightened at her sudden intake of breath. He kissed the palm of her hand and she snatched it away like the kiss had scorched her skin.

"Stop that," she hissed. "Please, listen."

Closing his eyes, Beckett tried to do what she asked, tried to ignore the heat thrumming through him still. He wanted to ignore her commands, to pull her tight against his chest and kiss her with everything he had.

"There, do you hear that?" She took a few steps down the street. Beckett followed her and soon he heard it too. A faint cry for help.

The street was lined with older houses in various states of disarray. Some looked unaffected by the storm but ravaged by the passage of time. One lot held a foundation with a single wall. Most were damaged, but still standing.

The farther they walked down the street, the louder the pleas for help grew. It sounded like an elderly woman. "Is anyone out there?"

"I think that's Mrs. Glass," Jess said, picking up her speed. She ran to a blue house three doors down from where they'd been. The house seemed mostly okay, if you looked at it only from the left. The walls on the right side had been ripped away, as if it had been built that way for a movie set or something.

"You think it's safe to go inside?" She paused at the stairs.

Nothing was safe about going into a house missing a side wall. If they called 911, would they even be able to send anyone, given the widespread destruction? Brushing that idea away as doubtful, Beckett steeled his nerves for what he knew he had to do.

"Help!" the shaky voice called from somewhere inside the structure.

"Do we have a choice?" Beckett asked. "Look around. Do you see anyone else on this street? It's us or nothing."

CHAPTER ELEVEN

JESS TROD CAREFULLY as she entered Mrs. Glass's damaged house. The floor creaked and with every step she took, the house gave off a shiver. The wind whipped around the open wall that was screaming its wounds into the breeze.

Beckett bumped into her from behind and the house gave a deep groan. His hands slipped around her waist. His touch remained gentle, steadfast. "Maybe you should wait outside. I'll find her and bring her out."

"She doesn't know you." Jess turned to face him, arguing the point. She'd known Mrs. Glass since she was five years old. "She might be hurt and afraid. A familiar face might make her calmer."

"She was my teacher too, Jess." Beckett waved his hand at the gaping hole where the exterior wall had once stood. "And even if she hadn't been, if this place collapses down around our heads, then it won't matter if she saw a familiar face or not, because we will all be in need of rescue!"

"Is someone there? I need help," Mrs. Glass called from the back part of the house.

"Beckett—"

"Will you go out there in the yard, *please*? If she can't walk, I can carry her out easier than you. I'll bring her out." He stuck his hand out, keys resting on his outstretched palm. The look in his eyes was what finally convinced her to let him be the one to go in. "Run back to the truck and get some basic supplies. If it collapses, I need you on the outside to go get help. Let me be the one to do this."

When she took the keys, he squeezed her shoulder and then disappeared behind the stairs. Jess didn't want to admit it, but he was right. It didn't make sense for both of them to be at risk in that trembling wreck of a once beautiful home. Being inside that damaged house was a dangerous choice.

Besides, there was Mason to think of.

She ran as fast as she could back to Beckett's truck. By the time she reached it, her calves burned from the exertion and her lungs reminded her that cardio was more necessary than she gave it credit for. Rather than empty one of the supply bins, Jess picked up Beckett's gym bag. She dumped the remaining contents on the floor and stuffed it with a variety of supplies. She left the AED. Mrs. Glass had been shouting, so Jess made a calculated decision that they wouldn't need it.

Swallowing hard, she tried to shake the guilt that stopping to help Mrs. Glass filled her with. She should be going straight to her son. But how could she have ever lived with herself if she'd continued and left that sweet elderly woman trapped, possibly injured and at risk of the house falling down on her? Stopping was the right thing, even if it was hard to convince herself of that at the moment.

As she ran back into the yard, Mrs. Glass's house gave out an ear-piercing screech and listed slightly toward the damaged side. A few loose shingles crashed to the ground. Oh, this was not good at all!

Jess stopped at the bottom of the steps. She peered into the interior of the house but couldn't see him or Mrs. Glass. "Beckett, it's not going to stay up much longer!"

Biting her lip, Jess agonized over what to do. Should she go in? Then they could all end up flattened like pancakes. With one foot hovering over the bottom step, she wavered on whether to risk going in to see if she could help somehow. Her desire to help warred with her self-preservation instincts.

"Beckett!"

"What's all the shouting about?" He appeared in the open doorway with Mrs. Glass held safely in his arms. The elderly woman was grinning from ear to ear. Shaking his head, he smiled down at Mrs. Glass. "You'd think she thought we were in danger or something."

Backing out of his way, Jess clung to the stone birdbath for support. In the emergency room, she was rock-solid. But when it came to the people she knew, the people she loved, those nerves of hers were less steady. Right now, she was on a tightrope looking down on her life. The only way to safety was a narrow path with danger on all sides.

And as much as it shamed her to admit it, that safety today was about six-foot-two and broad shouldered. She'd leaned on Beckett that day, even as she pushed him out to arm's length. She wasn't the lean-on-a-man type. Men were a luxury, not a necessity in her life. So, what was making this one so indispensable?

The fact that he'd saved her life? Because he had.

Even though she'd depended on his steady presence, she still wasn't sure that she could trust him. Could she ever really trust him, given her past? Maybe not. Depending on Clint hadn't gone well for her in the past. Although, she was already seeing that Beckett was nothing like her ex.

Beckett was kind, where Clint had been selfish. He was thoughtful, where Clint had been oblivious. Yes, they shared a similarity in terms of their financial situations in life, but every passing moment she spent with Beckett made her think that she'd misjudged him. Clint would never have risked his life for a complete stranger, but Beckett had not only done so, he'd done so after being given an out.

Still, it was only when he came out of that house, safe and sound, that she could truly breathe again. And she didn't want to evaluate that *why* any further. Chalk it up to an adrenaline-fueled connection, but for the first time in years, Jess could almost see a future with someone.

Beckett moved to the middle of the front lawn, easing Mrs. Glass to the ground. Before he could rise back up, the house gave out an eerie howl before imploding. A cloud of mothball-scented dust whooshed from the collapsing structure.

"Oh, my!" Mrs. Glass let out a sob. How much must it hurt to watch your home of fifty years reduced to nothing more than a pile of rubble? Jess knew that her former teacher had lost her husband a few years back, and now her home as well? What did she have left?

Jess's throat was thick with emotion thinking of all the elderly woman had lost. While she couldn't change the destruction around them, she could make sure that Mrs. Glass was physically okay. Jess sank down next to her. "Are you injured? Let me take a look at you."

Pulling her stethoscope out, Jess listened to Mrs. Glass's heart and lungs. Nothing sounded unusual. Her heart rate was up, and probably her blood pressure as well, but she was in her late seventies and had just been through something life-threatening and traumatic. Elevated heart rates were going to be the norm for a while. Jess was certain that if someone were to check her own vitals at the moment, hers would be high as well.

"I got trapped in the bedroom. I went back in there to get my sweater just as the storm hit. Something got wedged in the door. And then a chunk of the back wall fell into my shoulder." Her age-spotted hands shook, as did her voice. "This shoulder does hurt something fierce, but I'll survive. Be doing better if you help get me off this cold, damp ground before I catch my death though."

"We will look at your shoulder in a minute." Jess shielded Mrs. Glass's eyes from the light, trying to check pupillary response. "Did you bump your head?"

"Jessamine Daniels, I taught you how to write your name. If my head hurt, I would have said. I think I can tell when I'm injured or not. I may be getting old, but I'm not senile yet."

"It's a valid question!" Jess huffed. "And it may have been a long time since I was in your classroom, but I'll never forget how much you helped me after I lost each of my parents. Let me look after you, please."

Mrs. Glass wobbled a bit at Jess's plea, but she finally gave a nod. "Okay, but I didn't hit my head."

"Mmm-hmm." Jess moved around behind her former teacher. "Let's get this sweater off though because it looks like you might have a cut under there that's bleeding."

Mrs. Glass simply nodded.

Beckett gently helped her pull the sweater off the injured shoulder. The thin blouse beneath it had a large spot, bright red with blood. "Looks like the damage happened through the fabric, but the fabric seems intact at least. Should make for a cleaner cut."

"Hmm…" Jess murmured. "Mrs. Glass, we're going to need to slip your shirt aside so I can get a better look at that cut."

"Not out in this yard you're not!" the elderly

woman protested. "I can't have the whole neighborhood seeing these expired goodies."

Beckett chuckled. "How about in your car? Don't suppose you have the keys on you? It looks like it made it through the storm okay."

"I have them in my pocket," Mrs. Glass said, grinning up at Beckett like he'd just given her the world. "At least the car will give me a hint of privacy."

Beckett helped her to her feet and let her lean on him as he guided her over to the car. Jess swallowed hard. A man who was that sweet to the elderly and so good with kids couldn't be as dishonest as Clint, could he?

She let out a shaky breath and picked up the supply bag. Treat Mrs. Glass and then get to the school, she told herself. No time to think about what kind of man Beckett Wilder truly was. Priorities sorted, she climbed into the backseat with Mrs. Glass, asking Beckett to turn around and block the view from the opposite side. She eased the blouse off and the cut started bleeding afresh. She quickly stuck a clean gauze pad against the gash and applied pressure to slow the bleeding. "Cover yourself from the front with your sweater," she suggested.

Once Mrs. Glass had done so, she called out to Beckett that he was safe to turn around. He leaned into the car and asked, "How's it look?"

"Decent-sized gash. Started bleeding again when I pulled the fabric from the shirt away." She lifted the gauze and saw the blood well up in the wound again. "Still bleeding."

Beckett reached out. "I can apply pressure if you want to try some Steri-Strips?"

"Thanks." She dug through the bag and found some of the sterile strips to close wounds. "If you want to get another piece of gauze ready, I'll pour some of the antiseptic in and see if anything washes out. I don't want to try to close it up until I'm sure none of the fabric made it into the wound."

"Already on it," Beckett said, managing to rip the clean gauze wrapper open single-handedly.

"Ready?" she asked, holding the antiseptic up. "This might be cold. I'm sorry."

The elderly woman tensed but nodded. "Let's get it over with."

Beckett pulled the used gauze away as Jess began. Antiseptic poured into the wound and Jess caught the excess with another piece of gauze to keep it from running down Mrs. Glass's back. Thankfully, the bleeding had significantly slowed.

"It's looking better already!"

"Gonna need stitches though," Beckett said as he put the clean gauze over the freshly cleaned wound. "I'd also recommend a more thorough cleaning than we can give here in the backseat of a car."

"Agreed." Jess nodded at him. "Let me see if I can get a couple of these Steri-Strips on it to help slow the bleeding though."

Beckett watched her carefully, moving just as she needed him to and without requiring verbal instructions. Once they'd done as much as they could with their limited supplies, Beckett stepped away from the car and closed the door to allow Mrs. Glass privacy to get dressed.

"I like him," Mrs. Glass said as Jess helped her put the soiled blouse back on. Jess hated the idea, but the elderly woman didn't have anything else, and she was already complaining of the cold. "How's that sweet Mason doing?"

Jess had to fight back a sob. It would only upset Mrs. Glass to know that by stopping to help her, they were delaying reaching the children, including Mason. "He was smiling like crazy when I dropped him off this morning."

She stepped out of the car and swiped at her eyes before Mrs. Glass could see her tears. "Beckett, can you radio Mrs. Glass a lift to the hospital?"

"Already have. Can't get an ambulance, but they are having other city employees transport noncritical patients. They said it would be about ten minutes. I let them know that the end of the street by Main was blocked, so they'll be coming from the other direction."

"You think we can safely leave her?" she asked Beckett quietly.

"I don't see any signs of concussion. The bleeding isn't bad enough to worry about her bleeding out. Seems safe for us to continue on to the school."

Jess quickly told Mrs. Glass that someone was on the way for her and to watch out because it might not be an ambulance. She stuffed the unused supplies back into the gym bag. Now that she wasn't occupied with caring for Mrs. Glass, the fear and panic that Mason was hurt slammed into her chest like a wrecking ball.

If something had happened to Mason... If it was exacerbated because she had stopped to help someone else...could she ever forgive herself?

CHAPTER TWELVE

JESS HEADED DOWN the street toward where they'd left the truck. She didn't look back and Beckett found himself staring after her, admiring the sway of her hips. The woman made scrubs look sexy, and that was a feat.

No "See ya later." No "Thanks for the help today." Not even an "Adios." A thousand potential ways she could have said goodbye flashed through his mind, before it dawned on him that he needed to pick up his feet and go after her or find himself stranded. She still had his truck keys.

Was this woman going to make him chase her for the rest of their lives?

The thought gave him pause. The rest of their lives? When had he started thinking about Jess in the terms of having a future? Jess had made clear that her heart was surrounded by razor wire, and she wasn't interested in taking it down for him or any other man. And he wasn't staying in Woodvale, while she had a career here. Plus, there was Mason to consider.

All these things needed more thought than he had time to give. Something had shifted somewhere leaving him off-balance. He didn't like it.

"Hey, Jess, wait up." He hurried after her.

When he got close, he could see that she'd left so quickly in order to try to get her emotions together. The proof of her momentary lapse of control trekked down her face.

"Tell me about Mason." First grade, that was what, six? Seven? Most parents he'd met couldn't wait to tell anyone who'd listen about the amazing feats that their offspring had accomplished. His best friend had a new story every time they spoke, about what his daughter had said or done.

"Mason is my world. And if I were to lose him, I couldn't go on." She sighed and wrapped her arms around herself. "That's why I need to get to the school. I need to make sure he's okay."

There was a hefty weight in her words that resonated deep within Beckett's soul. He'd lost loved ones and it was a position he never wanted anyone else to be in.

The fear from the night Sloane died came back to him. The family had been told Sloane and her fiancé had been in a bad car accident, but they didn't have details. It had been one of the most terrifying moments of his life, as an eighteen-year-old on the cusp of adulthood. He had no idea how much those fears would be amplified if they were about your own child though.

"Come here," he said, pulling her into his arms. The need to comfort her overrode the self-preservation instinct that said touching her would only make his confusion worse when it came to Jess. "I'll get you to your son. That's a promise."

He just hoped the kid was okay when they got there.

CHAPTER THIRTEEN

ALLOWING HERSELF JUST one single moment of weakness, Jess let Beckett hold her. Being a strong, independent woman was her hallmark, but today was one of those days when she wanted a set of broad shoulders to lean against, some muscular arms around her and a deep voice murmuring reassurances in her ear.

God, why did Beckett affect her like that?

Restless butterflies fluttered around in her stomach at his touch though. Seeking comfort from Beckett Wilder, of all people, was such a dangerous proposition. She needed to be reinforcing the walls around her heart. Bubble-wrapping herself to cushion her heart from all the ways he could break it. Not snuggling into his chest and letting him murmur sweet reassurances in her ear.

Logic intervened and she sucked down a deep breath. She pushed Beckett away and fought down the rush of anger that surged up. Anger at herself, and the situation as a whole, since Beckett had done nothing but be supportive. She just needed to survive the next few hours in his presence without falling into his arms again. And she had to find a way to keep him and Mason apart. She couldn't get involved with Beckett and keep them separate forever, so she had to put the distance back between them. For Mason's sake, she couldn't let them bond any further...

"I need to get to my son," she said as she climbed back into his truck.

He looked pained at her brusque tone, but she had to focus. She couldn't let herself be swept up in a whirlwind romance. There'd been enough wind already, and like the devastation that the tornado had caused, Beckett had the power to devastate her heart. A stronger person would have never let him get this close.

Jess was ashamed of how much she'd started to rely on him today. This wasn't her. She didn't lean on others to get through the day. She faced problems head-on and without hesitation. People looked to her for an example of what to do. Jess had a reputation for being calm and collected during an emergency, and very few people knew her well enough to know that she did her falling apart after everything was over.

Being around Beckett was making her soft, and it couldn't continue.

After Clint, she'd vowed not to get involved with another man who held any sort of power over her. Wealth alone put Beckett in a vastly different league, and she didn't like the imbalance. There was something about Beckett's touch though that seemed to skip past all those red flags and strip her bare.

He reached over and picked up her hand. When he brushed his lips across the back of her wrist, she swore the temperature in that truck cab shot up a solid ten degrees. Man, it was hot in here. The way he looked at her, his eyes locked on hers, with his firm steady grip on her hand, holding her close, sent her internal thermometer sprinting up.

"I don't want to fall in love with you," Jess finally blurted out when she regained the ability to form words.

"Ah, Jess, I don't want to fall in love with you either." He looked right through her just then, it seemed like. Like he could see her every insecurity and wanted to put them to rest. "I don't know what happened to you in the past to make you so skittish around me, but I can see it in your eyes. My mind says stay far, far away. I can't seem to keep my distance though."

He had to be toying with her. Maybe he was looking for a hookup, because men like Beckett Wilder didn't get serious with single moms like herself. And her life definitely didn't have room for casual. "Are you considering coming home to Woodvale permanently?"

"No."

She pulled away from his touch. Breaking eye contact, she looked out the window. "Can we just get to the school, please? I don't have the right energy or mindset to deal with whatever this is right now."

Beckett turned back on Main Street. They drove two blocks down before either of them spoke again. "And if I was considering a move home? Why do I get the impression that it still wouldn't change anything?"

Shaking her head, Jess started to argue. Words failed her when she realized that Beckett had just turned onto her street and what might be waiting a quarter of a mile down the road filled her soul with dread. She hadn't given much thought to the state her own home might be in after the tornado.

"What's wrong?" He reached for her hand again, before giving it a reassuring squeeze. "You look like you've seen a ghost."

The level of attention he paid astounded Jess.

Women searched for that, but rarely found it. To be noticed was one thing, but to have a man so attuned to your expressions that he caught a mood shift in a split second... So very rare. Especially when they'd just been arguing, and he dropped it in an instant to be so supportive.

Stop thinking of him as a possible boyfriend, Jess admonished herself. Get through today, and he won't look so delectable. *Hopefully*. Waving her free hand up the street, she said, "My house is just up the way."

She'd already lost her car. Her place of work was severely damaged and might take months to repair. Mason's status was still unknown. And now she had to worry about their home.

"Can you see it from here?"

"No, it's just out of sight. Third on the right, just over that hill."

His thumb rubbed slow circles over the back of her hand. "And it just hit you that you don't know what we're going to find?"

Jess nodded. Fear clenched around her gut like a fist. Everyone had a limit. Where was her breaking point? Would she find it today?

"Yes." She swallowed hard. What if...? No, she couldn't keep dwelling on the negatives. It was growing harder and harder to focus on the positives though. She tended to be positive overall, but she couldn't bring herself to be that person right then.

"We're nearly there. Let's hope your home has been spared."

CHAPTER FOURTEEN

KEEPING THE TRUCK barely above a crawl, Beckett eased down the street. Debris blocked the lane in places, so it kept their speed greatly reduced. As they drove by, Jess commented on a few of her neighbors' houses, showing sympathy for the ones that had damage and expressing her relief for the ones that had escaped unscathed.

As they neared the top of the hill, she murmured. "I don't know if I can do this."

After stopping the truck, Beckett reached over and took her hand. He offered her as much comfort as he thought she'd accept. "You can. And I'll be right here beside you."

"What if the house is…?" She bit her lower lip and stared up at him, unable to verbalize the rest of that worry.

"Where's your bravery?" He teased a bit, trying to lighten the mood. Today had been a lot. Facing the potential loss of a child would be a drain on the strongest of people. Now her house as well? Jess was bearing up with a lot of grace.

"It blew away in the wind." She winced, and he could see that she hadn't meant to say that out loud. "That was far meaner than I meant it to be. I'm really not so weak as today might show. I'm sorry."

"I know." Beckett pressed his lips to Jess's forehead. He hadn't known her long, but he could already tell that she was one of the strongest women he'd ever met. It had to be rubbing her all kinds of wrong to feel weak in front of him. "It's fine. You're doing fine."

She took a deep breath, gathering strength. "Okay, let's do this."

He put the truck back in motion and they crested the top of the hill. She gasped when she got a good view of her house. It was still upright, but the entire roof was gone. The trusses and rafters, gone. Not a shingle in sight.

Shaky breaths that verged on crying but didn't quite cross over came from the woman at his side. "My house," she whispered. The single word carried a wealth of emotion—pain, fear and a hint of hope.

While Jess was giving her house a once-over, Beckett pulled out his phone and tried to call his parents. The call connected this time, but there was still no answer. He got their machine instead. *You've reached the Wilder residence. Please leave a message and we will return your call at the earliest possible convenience.*

"Mom, it's me. Call me back." He hung up and tried her cell. Straight to voice mail. Same with his dad's. He left a message for both that he was fine, asking for them to call him back and check in so he knew how they had weathered the storm. The lack of communication began to worry him. He fired off a text to each of them just in case they weren't getting the calls through on their end.

With that done, he turned back to Jess's house. The structure here seemed to be solid, thankfully. Badly damaged, but in no real danger of falling. At least to his untrained eye. The extent of his construction knowledge was limited to weekends spent working on a Habitat for Humanity house though, so he could hardly claim any expertise. The heavy rain would have drenched the exposed top floor, given that it was entirely open to the elements. If they were lucky, the downstairs would be salvageable, but even that was iffy. The house was in bad shape and wouldn't be inhabitable for a while.

He couldn't help her with the house, but he'd made her a promise to get her to her son. "Anything you need to grab before we go on to the school?"

CHAPTER FIFTEEN

BECKETT STOOD NEARBY, ready to take her on to the school. Thankfully, he was giving her a little distance. She'd already let him get far too close. Maybe when she got home tonight, she could put him out of her mind.

That was when reality hit her like a sledge-hammer right in the heart. Her home was destroyed. Yeah, the main structure remained upright, but the roof was completely gone. She sucked in a deep, ragged breath. There was no way they could live in that house.

"Oh, I…" Words failed. They were effectively homeless.

"We'll worry about where you're going to stay after we make sure your son is okay. He's the first priority." Beckett anticipated the topic dominating her thoughts.

"I know."

"Maybe your son can stay with his dad while

you get the house fixed? Or at least until you find some temporary housing."

"Not an option," Jess snapped.

"Okay then," Beckett stepped back, and Jess could see the hurt in his eyes. He'd had no way of knowing that his suggestion was completely unacceptable. After all that he'd done for her, he deserved better than her ripping his throat out over something so innocuous.

A few hours ago, she'd been dead certain that she was too good for the likes of Beckett Wilder, but maybe he was too good for the likes of her. She'd been a complete mess today, while he'd been a solid foundation, willing to let her lean on his strength. He needed a woman who was open and kind. She'd been none of those things, and yet he still stood by her side.

When she spoke again, the bite was gone from her voice. "My emotions are all over the place today and you seem to be my favorite target. It's just me and Mason now. My sister is a couple hours away. There's no one else he can stay with."

"You are under a lot of stress today, and I'm the safe target." Beckett gave a weak shrug, like it didn't bother him. But he stuffed his hands in his pockets, clearly still smarting from her biting his head off once again. "You ready to get moving then?"

Ten minutes later, they were pulling into the school parking lot. There were so many cars that Beckett had to park in the grass. As she took in the damage to the school, once again, the devastation was hard to bear.

Clutching at Beckett's arm, Jess let out a pain-filled gasp. "That's where Mason's classroom is…was." Seeing that large pile of rubble that should have been classrooms stabbed a shard of emotional glass down deep in her soul.

The notion that her little boy could be under all those broken bricks and shattered glass left a hollow hole in her gut. She swallowed hard, but the lump in her throat wouldn't budge. They should have been there already. She shouldn't have stopped to help others or to see whether her home was still standing. What if their delay had cost Mason his life or caused permanent damage?

"Let's find out who's in charge. Maybe we can get a status update on Mason and find out where we can set up to do any first aid that's needed." Beckett squeezed her hand.

Jess nodded. The only thing keeping her from a full-blown panic attack right now was Beckett's calm voice and the grounding his touch brought her. She didn't deserve his compassion, but she was thankful to have it. Her gaze jumped around, scanning the faces of all the crying children lined up along the sidewalk. They walked past class after class of children, none of which was the one she was looking for.

"His class isn't here." Her grip tightened on Beckett's hand. "Where is he?"

"We'll find him, Jess." Beckett's voice tried for reassuring, but he could no more promise that Mason would be healthy and safe than he could change who he was. One of the first lessons she'd learned working in the emergency room was to never make promises to a victim's family. Despite best efforts, things didn't always go the right way. And in a natural disaster situation with possible crush injuries, the risks were even higher that things wouldn't be okay.

"There's the principal." Jess headed over to a small woman in a wrinkled and dirty suit. "Mrs. Caruthers, I don't see my son, Mason. He's in Shannon Couch's first-grade class."

The principal visibly shrank, tears filling her eyes. "They're still in there. Rescue crews are still trying to get the kids out. We made contact with Shannon a bit ago. She said they were in a small void, but all the children are with her and there are no serious injuries. The problem is that the situation is volatile, and status could change in an instant."

Dread plopped down hard in Jess's stomach and sent up a wave of nausea that took some effort to swallow back. If she'd had more in her stomach, it might have ended up on Mrs. Caruthers's shoes. The fear she'd carried all morning, the worry that she'd been able to shove back as a mere possibility, was now a confirmed reality. Mason was missing. He was buried alive.

She sucked in a ragged breath. Mason was buried alive. Her baby was under a pile of rubble. The tightness in her chest nearly took her to her knees. She had to keep a grip, somehow. For Mason's sake, if not her own.

"How can we help?" Beckett asked. He kept his grip tight on Jess's hand, whether through an awareness that he was the only thing keeping her from spinning out entirely or as an attempt to keep her from rushing full steam ahead into the rubble she wasn't sure. "Jess and I want to help. She's a nurse and I'm an EMT. We have limited supplies, but what we do have is knowledge. We were sent over by Woodvale Memorial. Do you have a triage area set up yet?"

"There's been an ambulance in and out over there. A few of the teachers are doing their best." Mrs. Caruthers gestured to a corner of the playground. A lone swing squeaked ominously in the breeze. "The fire department ordered us not to touch anything on the building. Said we could make things worse if we went in wrong." She rubbed a shaking hand over her face. "We have thirty-three kids, two teachers and an aide still in there."

"Including Mason," Jess whispered. She didn't trust her voice at normal volume. If she tried to speak, and her voice cracked, that would set off the tears. She had to keep it together and stay strong.

Beckett led her away from the principal toward the place she'd pointed out as the designated triage area. He wanted to triage and bandage injured children? She just wanted to find her son.

"I don't know how to do this. How do I care for someone else's child when mine is buried alive over there?"

"You're a nurse, aren't you?" His low voice soothed her nerves the tiniest bit. "This is just another day in the ED. One patient at a time. Treat those babies like you'd want someone treating Mason if he was hurt."

They were heading toward a group of crying kids crowded around a couple teachers. The teachers looked overwhelmed, with hair sticking up in all directions and marks of dust and grime on their faces. Every one of them looked like they needed a savior. He was right that they did need to help the other kids. She could do nothing for Mason except wait, but she couldn't seem to wrap her mind around that. Around not being able to help her son.

"Start triaging these kids while I go grab our bins of supplies."

Jess nodded and let Beckett give her orders. She had enough mental clarity to know that she wasn't in the right mindset to lead. She introduced herself to the frazzled teachers and explained that she and Beckett were there to take over for them on triage. Their relief was palpable. One even cried.

She spent the next hour treating Mason's schoolmates. She put bandages on cuts, and even splinted a few potentially broken arms. She glanced frequently over at the front of the school, hoping for news, waiting impatiently for the rescue crew to dig Mason and his classmates out of the pile of ruin that was the first-grade hallway.

Beckett hovered close by, keeping a watchful eye over her. His nearness and concern made her feel protected. For the first time in her life, a man was watching out for her. It was nicer than she'd imagined. Somehow, she'd pictured anything with this level of power imbalance being, well, unbalanced. Experience had taught her that a man like Beckett should be overbearing, controlling her every move, right?

He wasn't like that at all.

Her relationships had been few, and even the most serious had never felt quite like this. Never had a man made her feel cherished just by the look in his eyes, or the way he put his hand on the small of her back when she needed a little extra support. What did it say about her past boyfriends if a man she'd never been on a single date with was more supportive than the lot of them combined?

Focusing on Beckett was the only way she could feel any emotion other than total fear. It helped keep her mind off the fact that her son was still buried, hopefully alive, only a few yards away. The distraction of providing first aid and the soft, gentle touches from the man at her side were the only things keeping her from curling up in a ball and sobbing until there were no tears left.

CHAPTER SIXTEEN

"WHY HAVEN'T WE heard anything?" Jess had asked at least once every ten minutes since they'd started delivering first aid to the students and teachers. Her lower lip was dark from how she was worrying it between her teeth.

"There's nothing yet to report," Beckett told her patiently. He wasn't a parent, but he could still find empathy for her situation. The knowledge that her son was still buried under the remains of the school had to be torture for her. "I know you want answers, but right now the best thing we can do is stay out of Search and Rescue's way and patch up as many kids as we can."

He was anxious and he'd only just met Mason. Low-level nausea roiled in his stomach every time he thought of how the bricks and stone that were currently giving Mason and his class a sheltered area could come down at any moment. Jess was bearing up fantastically, given how that thought had to be in the forefront of her mind as well.

Luckily, none of the children had presented with serious injuries that would have required full concentration. About half of the students had been picked up by worried parents, but they still had a few more to check out.

A little girl limped up to them.

"Hi, sweetie." The smile on Jess's face didn't reach her eyes. She was really trying—no one could fault her effort—but she wasn't quite succeeding. "What's hurting you today?"

They'd briefly tried a swap where Beckett treated the kids and she gave him the supplies, but her distraction had been far too great, and he'd ended up working alone. She'd told him that she needed to be working directly with the kids, to help keep her mind focused as best she could, so that was what they'd done. It was working fairly well. He didn't miss the constant glances over to the school though.

"Hurt my foot." The little one pointed down to a pink sneaker-clad foot. "Tripped over a rock."

"Okay, can you sit down here and let us take a look?" Beckett patted the dusty lid of a cooler that someone had dragged out of the back of their vehicle. They weren't using it for its intended purpose, but as a makeshift exam table.

The girl sank down onto the cooler and dutifully propped her foot up. She winced, but bravely held back her whimper when Jess eased the sneaker from her foot. A tear trekked down her cheek, leaving a muddy trail in the grime the day had left on everything.

"Light swelling." Jess manipulated the ankle slightly. "Does this hurt?"

"Yes," the child said with a hiss.

"Did it feel like anything cracked or did you hear a pop?"

"No."

"Okay. I think it's just sprained."

Beckett nodded when she looked up at him. He agreed it was likely a sprain from the looks of things, and it didn't change how they'd treat her today if it was broken. Without an X-ray or scans, the best they could do was immobilize it. He dug out the PT tape and some wrap.

"Mr. Wilder here is going to put some gauze and tape on that for you. It might still hurt, but this will keep you from hurting it more until your grown-ups can get you to see a doctor and maybe have a special picture of your bones called an X-ray done on it."

He'd been confused the first time Jess had referred to a kid's grown-ups. The look on her face when she'd explained to him that she never knew what a child's home life might entail had really dug deep into his mind. He'd had the ideal family, in a lot of ways, with both biological parents in the home and involved with his life. Overbearing, yes, but never abusive or cruel. He had an older sibling to follow behind. The idea that some kids had only one parent, some lived with other family or with virtual strangers, had never really been in his thoughts. He knew it happened, of course—he wasn't *that* naive— but it had never touched his life personally. Talk about feeling shallow and entitled.

His ignorance on that had probably reinforced Jess's opinions of him. He'd gotten the impression that Mason's dad had come from a wealthy family and wouldn't have concerned himself at all with the feelings of others. And if he was honest, his sister Sloane probably wouldn't have cared about hurting a kid's feelings if she asked about their mom or dad only to find out that parent was dead. For all her good qualities, his sister had been pretty self-centered. If Jess thought he was like that, that was probably why she kept him at such a distance. Hopefully, one day she'd be able to look at him and see him for himself. And stop comparing him to a man long gone.

"Let me see that ankle." He crouched down and turned his focus toward taping up the little girl's ankle. He'd just ripped the final piece of tape when Jess stood up and left.

"Make sure your grown-ups have a doctor look at that, okay?"

She nodded.

He waved to the teacher standing nearby and got her attention. "Can you keep an eye out? I need to see where Jess went."

As he walked in the direction she'd gone, he could see the SAR guys filing out of the school. He didn't see more kids though. A bitter taste filled his mouth. This wasn't good.

Jess stood in front of the school arguing with the principal and a member of the SAR team. To say that she wasn't taking whatever they'd told her well was a vast understatement. Her hands were planted firmly on her hips and the tension in her frame was visible from a distance.

"You can't just stop!"

He got within range to hear that last exclamation and caught the gist of the conversation. The SAR team was taking a break or stopping for some reason, and she wasn't having any of it. Beckett sucked in a deep breath. He wasn't sure he could find a way to smooth this over with her. It looked like she was far too fired up to be simmered down now.

Beckett stepped up next to them and tried to put a hand on the small of Jess's back. Her anger was too strong for her to allow the touch and she moved just out of his reach. The vibe around her was outrage, pure and simple.

"Ma'am, we aren't stopping. We need to get some more equipment brought in and my men need to get a meal and take a short break. If we had a second team, I'd send them in, but these guys are worn out. Most of them were out last night doing swift water rescues and haven't slept since night before last. If I don't give them a break, I'll need someone to rescue them."

Jess pressed her point hard. "My son is only seven years old. You have grown men who can't suck it up for an hour or two more?"

The SAR team leader scrubbed a hand over his eyes. Exhaustion deepened the lines of his weathered face. "You have to be worried half out of your mind. I would be. Trust me, we will do everything we can to get your boy and the others out safely and as quickly as we can without getting anyone else injured. You can stand here and yell at me 'til we both fall over, but those men are my responsibility, and they need to eat. They need to hydrate. Simple as that."

"Jess, they're doing the best they can," the principal argued. "This isn't easy for any of us. We're all worried, but the best thing we can do is to remain calm."

"Easy for you to say! He didn't stop looking for your child!" Jess jabbed a finger at the SAR leader.

"He hasn't stopped looking, Jess," Beckett tried to calm her down. It wouldn't do to make an enemy of the man leading the search team, and if she were thinking at all clearly, she'd see that too. "He's just making sure that his men are safe. They can't work if they're weak from hunger. Maybe you should think about going over and getting a sandwich yourself."

A local business had come out with sandwiches, bottled waters and some protein bars. They were handing them out to the kids still awaiting pickup and the adults there helping in various capacities. The SAR team that had come out of the school were currently all lined up getting themselves some food and much needed water.

"I'm not hangry," she growled out, her eyes flashing dangerously with anger as she turned her attention to Beckett. "I'm worried about my son."

"As are we all," Beckett soothed. It might have been a mistake to tear her attention from the SAR leader, but he had a better chance of getting her calmed down than the man she thought wasn't doing enough to save her son. "But it doesn't do Mason any good if his mom falls down from low blood sugar, now, does it?"

Her jaw tightened, and he thought she might continue to argue, but instead she stomped away over to the sandwich table. Her muscles were so tense that she'd be sore tomorrow, from the looks of things.

"I'm sorry." Beckett apologized for her. "She's normally much calmer."

"Worried mamas come with the job." The man shrugged and let out a little chuckle. "I don't let it get to me anymore."

"Good." Beckett shook the man's hand. "I appreciate the work you do."

Giving the principal a nod, Beckett went to get himself a sandwich. He had just walked up to the table when Jess moved away, sandwich in hand. His eyes followed her for a moment, content when she sank down in the shade of a tree to eat.

"Ham or turkey?"

"Turkey," Beckett said. "And can I have a few of those protein bars for later? I'm going to be here until all the kids are out."

The lady held two protein bars out. "Sure thing. Terrible thing, this, isn't it?"

"Beyond terrible." He took the proffered protein bars and stuffed them into his pocket. "Thanks."

After going over to Jess, he sat next to her.

She glared at him for a moment. When she didn't say anything, he started eating.

"You okay?" he asked between bites. She seemed even quieter than usual, and that worried him. Too much thinking might not be a good thing for her. There was far too much negativity today and he didn't want her to get too deep into a depressive mood.

"No."

The unshed tears in her eyes nearly broke him. "They will find him."

"What if it's too late?"

"Jess, you gotta have faith." Even as he said it, he knew it was easier said than done. "How 'bout we focus on something positive? Tell me something funny that Mason does."

"He has this obsessive desire for a dad." Her lip quivered. "At the ice-cream parlor the day we met, I was sure that he was going to propose to you for me."

"Propose?" Beckett laughed.

"Oh, yeah. He's done it before. Once, he went up to a complete stranger in the grocery store and asked him if he'd marry me so that he could have a dad."

Beckett snorted. "Well, since you aren't wearing a ring, I guess that didn't work out."

"The man was in his sixties!"

The question of why Mason didn't have a dad

burned hot on the tip of Beckett's tongue. Earlier, she'd said Mason couldn't stay with his father, but she hadn't elaborated as to why. He wanted to dig into that, get a deeper explanation. It seemed to be a touchy subject though and he didn't want to poke that bear again since she'd only just started to settle down.

"He's obsessed with baseball," she continued. "You might have noticed."

"I played baseball all the way through high school. Still play rec league when I can." It had been one of his greatest joys for a lot of his childhood, the one moment where he and his dad had found a connection. Baseball was high on the list of things Beckett hoped to share with his future children. He leaned back and tried to consider just when the idea of having kids had shifted from a maybe to a definite want.

"You know you've got superhero status with him." The smile she flashed him was bittersweet. She was dwelling on the what-ifs again.

He wanted to push those thoughts from her head—knowing they'd only build and grow to Jess's detriment—but he couldn't seem to find a way. The only thing he knew to try was to focus on happy things with Mason. To treat the future as a given.

"I'll happily play catch with him anytime he wants. Maybe show him a few pointers." Beckett put his hand over hers. He wanted to give her something to look forward to, something optimistic. "The three of us could even go to see a game?"

"We'll see."

Whenever his mom had said that growing up, it meant no. It was only second to *Let's see what your father thinks* in terms of ways she could say no without directly saying no.

"Is that universal mom code for no?"

"No."

Beckett let out a slight chuckle. "Why don't I believe you?"

"I'm going to throw away my trash." Jess stood and left.

Beckett finished the rest of his sandwich. When a cold feeling of dread dropped low in his belly, his eyes automatically searched for Jess.

CHAPTER SEVENTEEN

JESS RUSHED INTO the school, hopefully before anyone saw her. They'd said to stay out, but if the rescue crew wasn't going to find her son, she'd do it herself. She was a strong, independent woman. She could do this.

Some decisions she could agonize over for days, taking an exorbitant amount of time to make her choice. Others, like this, were made almost without any deliberation at all. This was pure instinct.

Physically, she couldn't wait any longer. Mentally, she knew it might not be the best choice, but that part had been overridden by the emotional part of her crying out that now wasn't the time to be logical. Now was the time for action.

"Jess," Beckett's voice called behind her. "What are you doing?"

Busted. She kept walking though. He could come with her or leave her be. She wasn't at his beck and command. Even if she'd accepted him taking the lead earlier, he wasn't her boss and he couldn't order her back like a wayward subordinate. Or sweet-talk her back either. She thought he was more likely to try the latter of those options. And she wasn't falling for either. She needed to find her son.

The inside of the school looked a lot like the emergency department had that morning. Glass shards littered the floor and insulation hung from the ceiling. At least in the spots that still had a ceiling. Some of the hallway was open to the blue sky.

"Jess, wait!" He caught up with her, grabbing her hand and tugging her to a stop. "This isn't a good idea."

"You're not going to stop me." She yanked her hand away and crossed her arms over her chest. Righteous determination filled her, and she rose up as tall as her petite frame would allow. "The only way you're getting me out of here is to carry me, and I'll be fighting you the whole way."

Beckett raised a brow at her. "You think I'm not capable of doing just that?"

Jess couldn't stop her eyes from traveling the length of his frame, taking in his broad shoulders and clearly toned chest. He absolutely could cart her out of here over his shoulder like a fireman. She swallowed hard at the images that carved into her mind. In another place, another time, she might not be opposed to the man going alpha on her and carrying her off to somewhere private. He was one-hundred-percent capable of taking her away from this wreck of a building.

A rush of panic that he might do just that rose up and she swallowed it back. Surely, he wouldn't take her away from her son when she was this close. "Maybe you can. I'm hoping that you won't though," she finally admitted.

He shook his head but didn't move to touch her. Even after spending the day with him, she had no idea what his thought process was like. The only thing she was sure of was that she'd been so far off on her estimation of him that it was like she knew nothing.

He'd been her rock today. And that had been entirely unexpected. Maybe, in a different time, a different life, they could have explored the attraction between them. But right now, she needed to get to Mason. She didn't have time for the push-pull of a potential new romance. And she certainly didn't have the patience for anyone getting in her way.

She'd used up every scrap of patience she had today. After a two-hour meeting with Beckett in which she'd felt like she had to justify every dime spent by her department, the hospital had been destroyed by a tornado during which she could have died. She couldn't dwell on how it had been Beckett who had saved her life. Then she had found out her son was in danger, and she'd had to convince Beckett to bring her along—okay, she might not have given him much choice, but it had tested her patience that she had to waste time arguing with him. She'd waited outside for hours, despite her intense need for action, while others tried to rescue her son and yet Mason remained trapped. The time for patient waiting was done.

Now she wasn't going to let Beckett or any other man stop her. She'd find Mason, if it was the last thing she did. "You can carry me out, but I'll just come right back in. I won't stop until my son is found."

Years ago, when she'd been dating Clint, she'd never had the courage to stand up to him for what she wanted or needed. He'd called the shots, decided who knew they were dating and where they went for dinner, even how they spent their time. She'd grown a backbone since then and when her son's life was at risk, the world had better believe she was going to use it.

"That I believe." A large sigh escaped him. "Okay, fine. We'll do this. But I'm coming with you."

"Just go home, Beckett."

"Not happening." He shook his head. "Even

if I were inclined to leave you to your own stubborn fate, which I'm not, I gave Freya my word that I'd take care of you. You may not know this about me, but I don't break promises."

She wanted to argue, but what would be the point? She could see the determination on his face and knew any efforts to talk him out of it would be futile. If he had one trait that she was certain of, it was his stubbornness. She had yet to decide if it was a pro or a con.

With a glance at her watch, she said, "Mason has been trapped for going on four hours now. We don't have a solid idea of where, or how much space they have, and worst of all, if they have enough air. I just can't wait anymore."

"That's why I said I'm coming with you."

"It could be dangerous." She squashed down an uncomfortable amount of guilt. Endangering Beckett seemed unfair. She absolutely could go on this journey alone. Should go it alone, even.

"And you think it's safer if you go by yourself?" Beckett tugged her up against his chest. He pressed a brief kiss to her forehead. "Woman, what am I gonna do with you?"

Why'd he have to be so sweet? She'd built Beckett up in her head to be a bad guy. He'd personified her own personal boogeyman who would come and break her heart. Mason's heart too. His actions had proven that she'd been entirely wrong in her assumptions about him though. Still, getting involved with him was a risk she wasn't sure she was brave enough to take.

"Let's go then," she said, pulling away from his embrace.

He wouldn't let her go entirely though, keeping his grip on her hand. Beckett had been generously sharing his strength and she was just selfish enough to keep accepting it for now. Soon though, she'd have to take that step back and stand without him again. It might be nice to have someone share the burden, but she couldn't put Mason through losing someone else he loved. Beckett was leaving, and she couldn't let herself get into the habit of depending on him.

"Left, I assume?" Beckett asked when they came to a T in the hallway.

Left led them toward the collapsed section. They turned the corner and at the very end, they could see the pile of rubble. There was a narrow pile leading up to it, where the SAR guys had been removing debris to pile it up out of the way. They hadn't managed to clear the hallway though.

"Mason's classroom is just past that blockage," Jess choked out. Visions of her son buried under those giant concrete blocks and chunks of ceiling and roof flashed through her mind.

Beckett's hand tightened on hers. "Positive thoughts only," he encouraged, but his voice sorely lacked enthusiasm. "Looks like we have our work cut out for us."

They proceeded quickly down the hall, intent on clearing the debris and finding Mason. After moving several big stones, a small landslide of debris slid down the blockage and knocked Jess off her feet. An ache sliced though her right ankle and she cried out in pain.

"Jess, are you okay?" Beckett placed the block he'd hoisted onto the excavated rubble and jogged to her side. "What hurts?"

"My stupid ankle," she groaned, clutching at the offending appendix. "I wasn't fast enough to get away. One of the bigger chunks rolled into it."

Beckett gently touched the ankle she indicated. "You think it's broken?"

"I don't know." She bit back a curse as he manipulated the joint and the pain intensified. "That really hurts though."

"Can you stand on it?"

"I'll have to try," she said with a whimper, allowing him to pull her to her feet. When she put her weight down on it though, she crumbled forward into his chest. "Nope. Don't think it will hold my weight."

Pressing her face against his chest, she fought

back tears. Mason needed her and she needed to be able to get to him. How on earth was she going to do that if she couldn't even stand up right?

"Hold on to the doorway here. Let me see if I can find something to make a makeshift splint or wrap with." Beckett helped her hobble into the closest still upright doorway. "I may have to run out and get a splint from the triage area though."

She'd only just told herself that she couldn't depend on Beckett, yet once again was leaning on his strength. It shocked her how much she'd already come to rely on him. And that was just foolish… The man had made it crystal clear that he was leaving town in only a few short months.

From the doorway, she could see that this was one of the second-grade classrooms. The interior of the room looked windswept, but significantly intact. Most of the posters still clung to the wall, although one corner of the one declaring that Second Grade Rocks was flapping in the light breeze. The only other sign that a tornado had hit this room was the far corner where a sliver of light came through via the missing roof and ceiling. Only about a one-square-foot space, sunshine beamed through it, highlighting that corner of the room like a spotlight, and providing the opening for the air moving the poster.

Beckett searched through the teacher's desk and the cabinet behind it. He moved on to the closet, carrying a roll of tape that he'd found in the desk. He pulled a sweater out and tossed it over his shoulder, still looking for something. When he turned, he had two rulers in his hands as well.

He held out his finds with a sort of grimace. "Not ideal, but I'm going to splint your ankle with this. Unless you want me to carry you outta here or go out and get a real splint?"

"No. They may not let you come back in." Or worse, they'd make her go out. Now that she was in here, closer to Mason, they'd have to carry her out under protest. Being near her son was something she desperately needed, even if she couldn't see or touch him.

"Didn't think so." He helped her over to the teacher's desk and lifted her up on it to sit. "Foot out."

Within a couple minutes, Beckett had used his scavenged sweater and rulers to tape her ankle. The snugness and extra support didn't take away all the pain, but the stability improved, and it did take the sharp edge off.

"I need to get that x-rayed," she admitted.

"Yeah, you do."

"Mason—"

"Comes first." Beckett tossed the remaining

tape onto the desk beside her. "But you have to take care of yourself too."

"Yeah," she said, brushing off his concern. She'd take care of herself once her son was found. Until then, she'd keep fighting to locate him until she physically couldn't.

Easing off the desk, Jess tested her weight on the ankle. She could stand to bear weight on it after Beckett's rudimentary splint, but only just. She hobbled back toward the hallway. A few times she had to pause because the pain washing over her was too much. The only things keeping her from curling up into a ball of defeat and bawling her eyes out were pure stubbornness and maternal instinct.

Before she made it to the doorway though, concrete blocks started to fall and the wall crumbled before her eyes. It happened almost in slow motion, like when a special effects crew played with the speed on a video to give a moment in a movie more impact. She'd never had that phenomenon play out in her own mind like that before, but it was unnerving.

"Jess, watch out." Beckett snatched her back and she landed on the injured foot. Pain shot through her like a lance.

When the dust cleared, Jess let out a curse.

CHAPTER EIGHTEEN

BECKETT PULLED UP the flashlight app on his cell phone and aimed it at Jess. The doorway she'd been headed toward was gone, filled with concrete blocks, ceiling tiles, wet insulation and a chunk of roof—at least from what he could tell now that the only light came from that busted ceiling corner opposite the door. That wall had come down fast and far too close to Jess for his liking. He shone the light up and down her limbs, searching her for injuries. "Are you hurt?"

The dust swirling through the air glittered under the artificial light from his phone. She coughed roughly as she inhaled some of those particulates. "It didn't hit me."

"Good. Try not to breathe too much of that junk in."

Once he verified with his own eyes that she was at least as whole as she had been prior to the wall's collapse, he angled the phone so that the light was aimed at their new impediments.

Once, there had been an opening in the white-painted concrete block wall, and now there was a tightly packed cluster of rubble. He was no contractor, but he could hazard a guess that the roof over that section of hallway had completely collapsed. Everything he could see looked like bad news.

"This is really bad, isn't it?"

He didn't answer yet. Moving closer, he used the flashlight to get a better look at the blockage. He pushed at the top, cautiously at first, then as hard as he could single-handed, but it didn't shift at all. Not even a pebble moved under his efforts. They were well and truly stuck. The question was for how long.

Stepping back, he rubbed at the nape of his neck. How could he tell Jess the only way they were getting out of here was by being rescued? And that their fate might be in the hands of the SAR team leader that she had shouted at less than an hour ago?

"Don't suppose you have a signal on that thing and can call us some help?" she asked, waving a hand toward the cell phone he held, its light still on.

He glanced at the screen. Zero bars and No Signal in bold print. "Afraid not."

Another potential complication was that his battery was down to less than 20 percent and he had no way to charge it. He would have to conserve what power he had left on the off chance he could get a signal later or in case they needed the flashlight again. He shone the light around the room once more, trying to get a feel for where things were and any resources that they might be able to scrounge up.

An idea sparked.

"If I can slide this desk over to that open corner, maybe I can break enough of that ceiling over there loose and see if there's a way out over there."

If it wasn't too dangerous...

"Oh, that would be great!"

"Honey, it's a risky plan that we can't bank our hopes on yet." Dismay rose in him. Was he giving her false hope by mentioning a potential escape plan? The chances that he could get out of that hole and have a stable space to drop down to safely were slim to none. But it was the only plan he had at the moment.

Afraid that he might see disappointment on her face, disappointment that he had put there, he shut the flashlight off without looking at her again. With a big shove, he got the desk moving and pushed it as far into the corner as it would go. After hoisting himself up quickly, he tapped at the wall as high as he could reach. It seemed solid enough, but the only way to find out if it could bear his weight was to jump up and grab the top.

The top he couldn't see.

There could be rusty nails, sharp slivers of glass or any number of things that could slice his hands right open. His back was still aching from the glass earlier and every movement exacerbated it. He had to try though, for Jess's sake. To be able to look her in the eye when the world stopped spinning and the smoke cleared, Beckett had to do everything he possibly could to get her to Mason.

Including the colossally stupid idea of trying to heave himself through a square opening roughly the size of his head. If he could at least get up there enough to get a good look, maybe he could come up with a better plan.

He'd always been good under pressure. It had been one of the things that made him a good EMT. He thrived under chaos, taking charge when others were losing control. He never cracked. All he needed was something to work with. What he was not great at was being patient and waiting for assistance.

Jumping up, he grabbed the edge of the exposed wall, leaving his body weight low and close to the desk. If it crumbled, that way he wouldn't have as far to fall. It didn't collapse. So far, so good. He pulled himself up. He could only just squeeze his head through the opening. If only Jess weren't injured, he could have boosted her up, but knowing her stubbornness, she'd vault right over into the unknown and injure herself worse—or leave him behind.

He could just squeeze his head through but couldn't get enough height to truly see anything. Dropping back down, he shook out his arms. It was a lucky thing he hadn't given up his conditioning routine after moving back to Woodvale.

"See anything?"

"Not yet. I'm going to have to try to peel back some of the roof and make the opening larger so that I can fit." He jumped back up, holding himself with one hand, and started to enlarge the opening. "Stand back. I have to toss this stuff down somewhere and I don't want to toss it out when I can't see what's out there."

He heard her shuffle backward. Once she was clear, he dropped a small piece of roof down on the floor next to the desk. He propelled back down and gave that arm a good shake. The next time he sprang up, he put his weight on the other arm. He alternated arms and bit by bit expanded the opening until he could fit his shoulders through. When he'd gotten up that morning, his biggest worry had been what tie to wear and how he could avoid the lecture from his mom about how it was time to settle down.

Now he was trying to fit his not so small frame through a hole in a ceiling while the dozens of cuts on his back protested as sweat trickled into them and burned. He would never have guessed how this day would turn out.

He paused for a moment, moving his arms in and effort to stop the trembling from all the pull-ups he'd just done. If he could have varied his grip, it might not have been so bad, but as it was, all the muscles in his arms twitched from the hardcore workout.

With one big jump, he was up again. This time, he hoisted himself up to waist level and looked down over the wall. He had to wait a moment for his eyes to adjust to the sudden brightness. Once they had, and he got a good look at what they were dealing with, he couldn't hold back the curse that slipped past his lips.

"What?" Panic laced Jess's voice.

He eased himself back down, not trusting the soles of his shoes on the slick top of the desk. Not the way sweat had been dripping off him. He sank down to sit on the desk. He couldn't see Jess as his eyes had yet to readjust to the difference in lighting inside the classroom.

"Can you come over here?" He wanted to be able to see her face more, so that he could better judge her emotions. So that he could ease her through this news if she took it badly—although he briefly wondered who was going to ease him through it. There'd been very few times in Beckett's life that a feeling of helplessness had overwhelmed him, and this was one of them.

The light pouring in from the opening above him highlighted her features. Even with a layer of dust on her cheeks, she was breathtaking. Holding out his hands, he wasn't disappointed when she stepped up and put her hands in his.

"Just tell me, Beckett. I have so many scenarios running through my head right now that it can't be worse than I'm imagining." Worry etched fine lines on her face.

"Behind me is just rubble. There's no way that we could jump down and not break an ankle." He frowned when he remembered that her ankle may already be broken. "Poor choice of words. You get what I mean though. It's a definite no-go."

"And the other side?" She still held a note of hope in her voice.

Hope that he was about to squash like a bug. "You know how the school has the walk-out basement?"

She nodded.

"This room is on the second story if you look at it from that side. With dropping from the roof, it would be a good thirty feet. It's not safe to try to jump."

"What do we do now?"

"Wait to be rescued, I'm afraid." Beckett rested his head on the top of hers. He wasn't a wait-to-be-rescued kind of guy, and he doubted that Jess was used to being slotted into the damsel in distress role, but the hole in the ceiling provided no viable escape route. The only doorway was blocked, and he'd been unable to get even a pebble to shift. Plus, they could make the collapse worse if they continued to dig at the blockage.

Jess stiffened in his arms. "Excuse me? Can you run that by me again?"

"You heard me." He rubbed his hands up and down her arms to try to soften the news. He couldn't keep the tension out of his voice though. "Do you have another idea? Any at all?"

His sharp questions seemed to throw her. His borrowed scrub top tightened as she clutched the material tight in her fist. Gently, he kissed her brow. So much for keeping calm. Good job, idiot, he rebuked himself. She was hanging on by a thread, so what was he doing letting his tone get so frustrated with her.

"Jess, it will be okay." *Somehow...*

The sun was beginning to set. Light that had once poured in and brightened the classroom took on an orange tint and the room grew dimmer with each passing minute.

"Mason has to be starving by now."

"I know." Even if the boy had eaten a huge breakfast, it was long past lunch. Beckett spared a moment of battery life to check the time. Six forty-five. They'd been trapped themselves for a few hours now.

"I'm getting hungry myself. Wishing I'd had two of those sandwiches now." Jess's stomach punctuated the comment with an audible roar. "Hopefully, they don't actually make us wait till tomorrow to get rescued."

Beckett pulled the protein bars from his pocket. He couldn't feed Mason, but at least he could make sure Jess had something to keep her going. "I had a feeling we might want something more than a sandwich. If I'd known how prophetic that feeling was, I'd have asked for more than two."

She took one and let out a shaky breath. Tears leaked out of her eyes, but she didn't sob. Her breathing was far more rapid than he would have liked, though, and she had a look in her eyes that sent a chill down his spine.

Before he could react though, a whirring noise from the vicinity of the collapsed wall distracted him. He turned the flashlight on again and watched as a large drill bit came through the still solid section of the wall. It backed out and a ray of light came through the small opening it left.

"Hello?"

"We're here!" Beckett and Jess chorused.

"You two safe in there?" the SAR team leader asked through the hole.

"Yeah," Beckett answered for them. "We're okay. Plenty of room, no worries about air."

"Okay, good. Well, I've got some good news, and I've got some bad news." He paused, and Beckett wasn't sure if it was for dramatic effect or just because he didn't know which to share first. "The good news is that this collapse that the two of you caused kicked out another wall which freed Ms. Couch and the kids. They're all fine, just some bumps and bruises. Getting fed right now. The bad news is that it's gonna take us all night to dig through this crap. Any chance you can see another way out?"

"There's a hole in the roof along the outside wall. Big enough we could squeeze out, but too high to jump off."

"Lemme see if I can get a crane out here then. Maybe we can hoist you out of there. Sit tight. And don't cause any more collapses." The light disappeared.

CHAPTER NINETEEN

"DID YOU HEAR what he said?" Jess sniffed. Relief coursed through her. "The kids are okay. Mason's okay."

She could finally breathe for the first time in hours. Truly breathe, as the weight that had been pressing on her chest lifted. Her greatest fear was to lose her son. Knowing that he was safe, that meant everything.

"That's the best news I've ever gotten in my life." Beckett's arms slipped around her waist and pulled her up to his chest. "Is parenting always so hardcore? I haven't even known the kid a week and I've been half sick to my stomach all day worrying about him."

"Worse," Jess confirmed. "Were you really worried about Mason? You barely know him."

"I was. I know it doesn't make sense, but I really feel a connection to that little boy. The thought of losing him...it just tore me up inside."

She tiptoed and brushed her lips against his. "That's just the sweetest thing."

He returned her kiss, lightly at first, then deepening when she shivered and moved closer. "You want me to stop?" he whispered against her lips.

"Mmm," she murmured, wrapping her arms around his neck. Anything else he might have said was cut off by her lips pressing against his.

Tracing his thumb lightly along her jawline, he kissed her gently. Sparks flew between them, kindled by mutual physical attraction, until it was a raging inferno. After easing back on the kiss, he brushed his lips over the hollow of her temple.

"When we continue this, I want it to be some- where safe, somewhere private and somewhere respectable. Not on a dirty desk in a disaster- damaged school." Beckett buried his face in the crook of her neck. "But don't doubt that I want this. I just want more for you than this."

She sighed and leaned into his embrace.

Hands skimming up and down her back, Beckett held her close. Even just this mostly innocent touch kept her fired up. She wanted to take this further, but he was right that it wasn't the right moment. Even though she wanted it, she knew it could never be anything more than a few stolen kisses in the dark.

Guys like Beckett didn't go for single moms like her. Why would he give up his freedom and his career for her? He wouldn't...

"So, now what?" Jess asked.

"Well, we might as well get comfortable. We may be here for a while." Beckett sighed. "Along the far wall is probably the safest spot. We should probably settle in before we lose all the light."

"I hate this."

"It's not exactly my favorite place either." Beckett gave her a little squeeze. "The company is growing on me though."

Her heart raced at his words. Several times that day, he'd said something along those lines, and she'd brushed it off as flirtatious attempts to relieve some tension. Now she wasn't so sure. Maybe it was wishful thinking on her part, but she thought he actually meant it. She desperately wanted to believe this was more than an itch to scratch for him.

"At a loss for words?" he asked, nuzzling his face into her throat.

"Today has been a lot to process." So much to process. Even now, she was trapped and couldn't see her son. She had to take the SAR leader's word that Mason was safe and sound. That nagging little worry in her gut wouldn't ease until she could see him for herself, but at least the crushing weight was off her chest.

With the worst of the worry about Mason gone, now she could focus on the man currently holding her so tenderly. Beckett had been a real surprise. She'd expected him to be like Clint, but other than their backgrounds, she couldn't find many similarities.

His breath was hot against her throat as he murmured, "Mason's safe now. We are all going home safe."

"But I'm pretty well homeless." She closed her eyes, her throat tightening as the thought rushed in. That house was all that she had left of her mom. And it was wrecked. The water damage alone was probably astronomical. Her insurance was up to date, at least, so the financial burden wasn't her biggest worry.

She needed to figure out where they were going to stay in the immediate future. And the sentimental loss of all her mother's things. All Mason's things…

"We'll figure it out."

There he went with the "we" again. She sighed. "There is no 'we' though. You keep saying 'we,' and the more I hear it, the more you make me want to believe that you mean that."

"I do."

"You know, following me in here and spending the night alone with me is going to make the town paper." The locals would have a field day with this. There was nothing a small town liked more than some juicy gossip about what man was sneaking into what woman's bedroom at night. Or, in their case, who got trapped together alone overnight. No matter how much she proclaimed that there was nothing between Beckett and herself, the black-and-white evidence would be hard to refute. "The article in the paper…" She trailed off without finishing her thought.

"Might as well serve as an engagement announcement?" Beckett chuckled. "I remember all too well how the gossip train works around here. Let them think what they want."

"Easy for you to say when you're leaving town in a few months." Jess feared her response sounded a bit strangled. When Beckett didn't seem to notice, she pulled away from his warmth. She wrapped her arms around herself, trying to recapture the heat but fearing that the chill wasn't physical. "You won't be the one getting all the side-eye glances and hearing the whispers stop when you walk in a room. I've been there and really don't want to go back. You'll be back to your normal life while Mason and I try to pick up the pieces and remember how to live life alone again."

"Is that what you're really worried about? Me leaving?" His fingertips grazed her arm as he reached for her in the dark. "What if I stayed? Would that change your mind about there being an us?"

"You've made it clear that your time in Woodvale has an expiration date."

"This place is home to you, right?"

"Yes," she said softly.

"I don't feel like I have a home. After I lost my sister, things here deteriorated rapidly. My father and I...well, we've never had the best relationship. But Sloane, she had a magic touch with my dad. She could charm him into anything she wanted—even cutting me a little slack." The sound of Beckett grinding his teeth reached her ears. Pain laced his voice when he spoke. "Without her, his expectations for me grew exponentially. No human could meet that man's criteria for what it means to be a Wilder. I couldn't wait to get as far away from that as I could."

"I'm sorry," she whispered.

"I know you see a spoiled rich guy when you look at me, but that's not who I am. Maybe I've never had to go hungry or worry about how I'll pay for a car repair, but that doesn't mean my life is free of hurt and struggles."

"I'm starting to see that." She'd hurt him with

her prejudice, something she'd never meant to do. When his fingers grazed her hand again, this time she entwined her fingers with his. They stood, close but barely touching; only the fingers of a single hand kept them connected.

Outside, the noises dwindled off and Jess wondered if everyone had gone home to get some sleep. The only noise for a while was the sound of their own breathing and the ribbiting call of a nearby frog.

"So, what if I stayed?"

CHAPTER TWENTY

JESS'S FINGERS TENSED in his. While he couldn't read her expression, he could feel the anxious energy radiating off her. She tried to be casual, to pretend that she wasn't interested in dating at all, but he could see through that thin armor. She had been hurt, badly. And he had a good idea that Mason's dad was the culprit simply based on her responses to him and his background.

But he wasn't that guy.

"Woodvale isn't what you want though," Jess finally replied.

A few weeks ago, she'd have been one-hundred-percent correct. Then he'd met her and Mason. He wasn't going to claim love at first sight or anything that cheesy, but there was a connection. A longing to be with them that almost made him want to throw aside his previous beliefs about Woodvale and give his hometown a second try.

Or better yet, maybe he could convince Jess to follow him when he went back to work. She'd said herself that she had no one here really. Maybe he could persuade her to relocate. Now, there was an idea he could really work with. With her house destroyed, what did she have to keep her here?

The idea would be one he'd have to ease her into though. No use bringing that up at the moment. He rubbed his thumb slowly over the back of her hand. "Maybe the people in Woodvale are growing on me."

"The people?"

He could almost hear how she'd raised a brow at him in amusement. "Okay, so there's this kid…" Mindful of her injured ankle, he moved closer to her. Slipping his arms around her waist, he turned her toward him. "He's pretty amazing and actually thinks I'm great. He and I…we're gonna be BFFs by next week."

She snorted. "Oh, yeah? Is that so?"

"Yeah." He sought her lips, tempting her, teasing her with a ghost of a kiss. "And I shouldn't even tell you how crazy his mom makes me."

"You are an incorrigible flirt." Her soft laughter filled the space.

"Maybe, but you're starting to like it."

"I will neither confirm nor deny that statement."

Beckett cradled her face in the palms of his hands and captured her lips with his own. Her reply was confirmation enough for him that she was getting over whatever obstacles she'd put between them. Each stroke of his lips over hers made him ache for more. Every caress of her hands across his shoulders reached deep into his soul and soothed the ragged edges that years of being afraid to love had created. Never before had he considered a long-term future with a woman. It was as if he'd been waiting his entire life for the right woman—this woman.

He'd been with his share of them, but never had he felt like this before. And Jess was unlike the partners he normally chose. If anyone had asked him if he'd ever get involved with a single mom, the answer would have been an emphatic *No way!* Yet here he was. Not only was he getting involved, but he was also the one doing the pursuing. Attracted or not, Jess would have let him walk on by, never engaging, never exploring the chemistry raging between them.

The vibe between them had him second-guessing his long-held opinions about this town and that had to mean something. The urgency he felt around her scared him a little. Something about her drew him in like gravity though, and he was powerless against the pull.

He was a person who valued control, who

needed to have choices and options. But the thought that he didn't have a choice when it came to Jess fled his mind as fast as it landed when she shifted closer. Her soft curves pressed into the firmness of his muscles, and the fit was perfection. He could get used to this.

"Mmm…" She tore her lips away from his with a gasp. Her hands applied firm pressure to his chest as she put a little space between them. "This is amazing, but we are moving a bit fast for me. I haven't done this in a long time and it's overwhelming."

Beckett groaned but allowed her to pull away. Things weren't moving fast enough for him. He knew what he wanted, and that was Jess. Fumbling for his cell phone, he murmured that he was going to turn on the light. They needed to find a spot where they could relax some and maybe get some semblance of rest.

"That corner right there looks like our best bet," he said, pointing at the farthest corner away from the collapsing wall and open ceiling. He scanned the room quickly, but there was nothing they could use to soften the tile floor or use to stay warm. The spring days had been warming up nicely, but the nights still got quite chill. "We will have to rely on each other's body heat to stay warm tonight. Hopefully it doesn't get too cold."

If it did, they'd be in real trouble. They'd survive without more food, and without water, until morning. But if it got below freezing, they'd have bigger concerns than being hungry or thirsty. He sat down in the corner and patted the floor next to him. "Might as well get comfortable. My phone's almost dead, so I think this is the last of the light."

She hobbled over to him, and he helped her ease down. She snuggled up against him and released a contented sigh when he anchored her to his chest with his arm. Jess acted like she was a loner, that she didn't need anyone else, but the way she reacted to him and leaned on him told a different story.

"Can I ask you something?"

"We're stuck together for the night. I don't think you need to ask permission to ask me questions." One of her hands trailed across his chest in a slow, deliberate pattern. "Ask away."

"What happened between you and Mason's dad?"

She sucked in a breath and didn't exhale for a very long time. He thought she wasn't going to answer and was ready to apologize for overstepping when she finally let that breath out. Tense in his arms, she hesitated before answering.

"Mason thinks he died."

"Did he?"

She sighed. "No. I... I told him that because it was less painful than telling him that his father had no interest in parenting him. I thought I'd found the man I'd spend my future with, and it turned out that I was simply a summer fling for him."

"Ouch..."

"Yeah. I excitedly told him that I was pregnant, and he told me that I had two weeks to clear out of our shared apartment. When he blocked my calls, I didn't know what to do next. So, I tried to tell his mom, thinking maybe she'd be able to talk some sense into her son."

"And that was a no-go?"

"She accused me of being a gold digger out to ruin her son's name. Like your parents, they were big boosters at the hospital where I worked at the time. She made me a deal—leave quietly with a good reference or she'd destroy my reputation both professionally and privately. I tried to stand my ground, but it was less than a week later that I was called into the HR office and let go. I moved home to Woodvale and never tried to contact Clint again. Mason's better off without that in his life."

Beckett ruminated on her words. No wonder she had built such walls. He embodied everything that had hurt her in the past. Even if he stayed in Woodvale, would he be able to convince her to take a chance on him?

CHAPTER TWENTY-ONE

"HELLO, IN THERE?" a voice called.

Jess stirred from an uneasy slumber, rubbing the sleep from her eyes. She tried to ease away from Beckett, but he had a solid grip on her in his sleep. She'd snuggled into his chest last night like he was her security blanket and they'd happily shared body heat and more than a few kisses and intimate confessions.

She still couldn't believe she'd told him everything that had happened with Clint.

"Beckett," she said, prodding his chest with her palm. "I think we're about to be rescued."

"Hmm," he muttered, his arms tightening around her.

"Hello?"

"We're here!" Jess shouted, her body still pressed to Beckett's since he had refused to release her.

His eyes blinked open since she'd just yelled practically in his ear. The fog of sleep still clouded his eyes. "You're loud," he said in a sleepy murmur.

"Someone's out there." Jess waved vaguely behind her. "I heard them."

"Try up here, lovebugs," the voice called again. The search-and-rescue leader peeked in from the hole Beckett had enlarged. The morning light created a halo around him. His flashlight passed over them.

"You two look nice and cozy. Maybe I should give you a little privacy and come back in a while?"

"Go ahead and tease," Beckett said with only the slightest of grumbles. "But if you're coming back later, could you at least bring us some food and water first?"

"I'll have you out in a jiffy, assuming you two don't mind scaling down the side of the building over here."

"We don't mind that at all, if there's safety gear. But I think Jess's ankle might be broken."

Jess let Beckett speak for them both. She'd found herself tongue-tied at the first tease that crossed the SAR leader's lips. Lovebugs? Was that what they looked like? Her lips turned up at the thought. Given that they had been asleep in each other's arms and hadn't separated even after awakening, she supposed that was a logical conclusion.

"I'll be right back with the gear."

"Wait!" Jess found her voice. "Any news on the first graders? I know you said you rescued them, but do you know anything about my son, Mason?"

"I only know that we were able to get them all out with only minor injuries. Not sure which one is your boy, so can't say for sure." Jess didn't miss the silent scold in the man's words. Her rash actions had caused more work for the SAR team, and she'd put Beckett in danger too. Still, she couldn't say she wouldn't risk it again. A mother's love was a mother's love. She'd do almost anything for that boy.

Mason was safe though. Even if she couldn't see him yet, he was safe. This whole ordeal was finally almost over. Soon, she'd be able to hold her sweet baby boy in her arms and she might never let him go again. Tears trekked down her face at the relief that realization brought.

"I told you to have faith." Beckett rubbed her back gently, murmuring those sweet reassurances. His steady voice and presence gave her exactly what she needed to pull herself together.

"I don't need any 'I told you so' from you." She nudged him and pulled away from his embrace.

He reached up and smoothed her hair. "You might need to use the bottom of my shirt to wipe the mud smears off your face though. Currently, you look like a cross between a raccoon and the chick who gets chased through the woods in a horror film."

Forty-eight hours ago, she wouldn't have cared what Beckett thought of her looks, but she hoped maybe after all they'd been though that he'd cut her a little slack. She knew she wasn't a supermodel, but she had been happy with how she looked. Her self-esteem hadn't been fragile. "Gee, thanks," she said dryly to cover the hurt his words had caused.

"I don't think that came across how I meant it to." Beckett tipped her face up to look at him in the dim morning light. "I think you're stunning, even when you have dirt on your nose and rivers of tears in the dust on your cheeks. But you might want to wipe some of that off before Mason sees that you've been crying. That's all."

"You are too perceptive. I'll never be able to keep anything from you, will I?" She struggled to her feet, trying to put a bit of distance between them. Beckett saw through her, like straight down to her soul. It was a bit unnerving.

"A spot clean should be enough to get some of this muck off you." He stood next to her and whipped the scrub top over his head. He flipped the shirt inside out and used it to wipe her face. His gentle, firm touch reminded her of her father. Once, many years ago, her dad had taken her to the county fair. She'd tripped and fallen face-first into a puddle. He'd used the inside of his shirt to clean her face just like Beckett was doing now.

"You'd be a great dad." The words slipped out before she could think about filtering them. She wanted to recall them the moment they crossed her lips, but the sentiment was true. He would be a great dad, just like her dad had been.

The hand holding his shirt fell down to his side. "You think so?"

She nodded.

"Good." He brushed his lips across hers. "In case you forgot, I kinda have a thing for this hot single mom. Think that earns me some bonus points?"

"Hmm…" She moved closer to his bare chest. "I think just taking off your shirt might earn you all the bonus points you need."

"I really can come back," the SAR leader said with a laugh from above them.

Jess choked back a laugh and pressed her face against Beckett's chest. This was getting ridiculous. Were they back in high school getting busted kissing in the stairwell?

"Nah, man, I think we can postpone this until after you get us out of here." Beckett answered for them. He stepped back from Jess and slipped the dirty shirt back over his head. "To be continued?" he asked in a low voice that only Jess could hear.

She swallowed hard. A fear settled over her that once Beckett laid eyes on Mason again his relationship with her and with Mason would be tainted by his newfound knowledge of Mason's paternity. Would the sweet connection they'd found within the broken walls, of this damaged classroom carry over into the light of day?

"Jess?" he prompted softly.

She could only nod.

"Okay, which one of you two lovebugs wants to go first?" The SAR team leader lowered a harness and it dangled over the desk.

"She's going first." Beckett guided Jess over to the desk and lifted her up onto the surface with ease. "Watch her right ankle. I splinted it as best I could with the limited resources I could scrounge up."

"Can you harness her up or do you need me to drop down?"

"I got it." Beckett fastened the buckles on the harness around her. He tightened them carefully, checking each one before he nodded. "She's ready."

"Beckett," Jess said softly.

"I'll see you on the outside."

"We weren't in prison." She snorted.

"Go see your boy. I'll catch up in a few."

The SAR team pulled her up slowly, and she watched Beckett's face as she ascended away from him until she was up in the open air above the school and the contrast in light made it too hard to see him. When she looked around after clearing the opening to the classroom, her heart started racing as it dawned on her that the ropes they were on were attached to a crane. He'd actually been serious about getting a crane! Somehow, she'd imagined that the SAR guy had just scaled the side of the building or something.

"Don't worry—there's not enough rope for you to hit the ground." He grinned at her. "Although, I think maybe we'll lower you down and then go for a break before we unstrap you."

"Ha-ha." Jess faked a laugh. He might be teasing her because of her attitude yesterday, but she wasn't sure of anything at the moment. "If I apologize for running my mouth yesterday, will you let me all the way down and point me in the direction of my son?"

"I was only messing with you a little." They reached the ground and he moved quickly to release her from the harness. "I'll be going back for your boyfriend now. But if you want to go around the side of the building there——" he pointed at the still upright section of the school "—you should see a small red tent there. I believe your boy is waiting there. If not, they will know where he's gone."

"He's not my... Thank you." Denying that Beckett was her boyfriend had been on the tip of her tongue but, given that the man had caught them kissing and cuddling, there was no way he'd believe her anyway. She hobbled toward the end of the building. At this point, she was functioning purely on stubbornness and the desperate need to lay eyes on Mason. Every step she took was agony as pain radiated through her injured ankle.

The uneven ground stretched before her like a never-ending obstacle course. Still, she kept going, because Mason was just around the corner of that building and she wasn't going to stop until her boy was back in her arms where he belonged. Adrenaline must have given her energy, because her last two meals had been skimpy at best.

"Need a lift?" Beckett's voice startled her as he swept her off her feet.

"They got you out faster than they got me." She wrapped her arms around his neck. Maybe she wasn't quite done relying on him yet.

"Nah, you just walk slow." He shifted her

position in his arms. "Where we headed, limping beauty?"

"Red tent," she said, waving a hand toward the temporary structure in question. "You don't have to carry me. I can walk."

"Sorta," he said with a laugh. "I hardly think that shuffle you were doing counts as walking. And what if I wasn't ready to let you out of my arms just yet?"

"Fair enough." She put her head down on his shoulder and let him carry her the remaining distance to the tent without protest. There was time enough later to get used to life alone again.

"What?" he asked.

"How do you do that?"

"Do what?"

She sighed. "Catch on to my thoughts almost as fast as I have them."

"You were relaxing in my arms and suddenly tensed up." When they reached the tent, he carefully set her back on her feet. "Even an idiot could notice the shift in your mood."

Before she could formulate a reply, she heard the sweetest voice in all the world call out a tentative, "Mommy?"

"Mason!" She spun so fast that she nearly lost her balance. Beckett steadied her while she embraced her son for the first time in over twenty-four long hours.

First, she squeezed her baby tight, only releasing him when he said he couldn't breathe. Then, she scanned every visible inch of him for injury. He was a filthy little thing, but other than a small cut on his forehead and a scrape on one arm, she couldn't see a thing wrong with him.

"You're really okay?" she asked, trying not to cry.

"Yeah." He looked down at her ankle. When he made eye contact with her, she could see the questions and a hint of exasperation in his blue eyes. "But you aren't. Mommy, how did you get hurt when my school fell down and I didn't?"

Beckett chuckled behind her. She elbowed him and smiled in satisfaction when his laugh became a grunt.

"Do you know how she got hurt, Mr. Wilder?" Mason decided to bypass her entirely and take his questions to someone else. "And why were you carrying my mommy? Are you going to get married now?"

"Mason," Jess hissed. "What have I told you? You can't just go around asking men to marry me."

Mason rolled his eyes and turned his attention back to Beckett. "You see what I have to work with? I'll never get a dad at this rate!"

Jess kind of wished that she could just go

back to that isolated dark classroom for a minute. At least in there, no one could see the visible signs of her embarrassment. She had warned Beckett about this at least, but it didn't make it any less mortifying.

Beckett laughed and ruffled Mason's hair. "I was carrying her because of her hurt ankle, which she got while trying to dig you out. Now that we know you're okay, what do you say to taking your mom to the hospital and getting this ankle looked at? I think she'd better have an X-ray on it and get a real splint or maybe even a cast, don't you?"

Mason nodded like he and Beckett were actually making plans. She kept waiting for the moment when Beckett decided that being involved with a single mom was too complicated. It was coming; she knew it was. And each of these moments where Beckett grew closer to Mason would only make that break harder.

"When the two of you have finished making plans for me, I'd like to get out of here," Jess grumbled. Her stomach let out an audible growl. "Have you eaten, baby? Mommy is starving!"

Mason pointed across the grass. "That lady over there has muffins. I think she likes me. She gave me two chocolate muffins and said I could have a blueberry one if I wanted after I finished those, but I got all full from that."

"Mom!" Beckett shouted happily, leaving their side to rush over to Mrs. Wilder who was standing with a huge basket of muffins in her arms.

CHAPTER TWENTY-TWO

"BECKETT!" HIS MOM TURNED at the sound of his voice. "What are you doing here? I've been trying to reach you since yesterday. Your father's gone to the hospital, thinking you were there. But when I heard there were still rescue efforts here, I felt I was needed more here."

He embraced her tightly.

"Darling, as much as I'm happy to see you whole, what are you wearing? I presume that you are aware of your need for a shower." She hugged him back briefly, but then pushed against him. "Don't share your stench, please."

Beckett laughed and tapped a finger to his mother's wrinkled nose. "This stench was the result of being trapped all night in that school and trying to dig my way free."

"Why were you in the school?" Confusion filled her eyes, along with a touch of concern. "If you hadn't left those messages that you were okay, I'd have really been concerned. You are all we have left now."

"I know, Mom." Guilt over worrying his mother rose up in him. After all that she'd been through, he hated to add to her pain. How could he explain that he was trying to spare another mother the trauma she'd gone through without reopening the wound of losing a child? It had taken his mother a long time to seem okay after Sloane's death. He didn't want her to backslide and get tangled in that web of grief again.

He turned to look for Jess, wanting to introduce her to his mother. She was still over by the red tent with Mason. She kept glancing his way. When they made eye contact though, she let her gaze drop quickly to the ground. That seemed unlike the bold Jess that he knew.

"Come on. There's someone I want you to meet."

"Oh, really?" His mom perked up. He could see the wedding plans in her eyes already. "That beautiful young woman talking to little Mason?"

"Yes, but please keep your cool. I haven't even taken her on a date yet."

"I'm going to take that as a hopeful sign that you want to though. That Mason is such a sweet child." And he was starting to regret that he'd offered to introduce her to Jess. She'd been angling for grandchildren for ages now.

"Jess," he said softly as they walked up. "I'd like you to meet my mother."

"It's nice to meet you, Mrs. Wilder. Your son has been a big help to me over the last twenty-four hours." She smiled softly at him, looking a bit shy. "I don't know what I'd have done without him."

"You'd have managed." He reached out and tucked a bit of hair behind her ear. "You're strong. I'm glad I could help though. Now, we need to get that ankle x-rayed."

Jess gave him a look. "I'll get it looked at. I promise. You can go now. You don't have to worry about me anymore." She hugged Mason tight. "I have everything I need now."

Beckett took a couple muffins from his mom's basket and held one out to Jess. "Except you haven't eaten since yesterday and you're only standing because of a sweater and a couple rulers."

"Rulers?" Mason squatted down to look at his mom's ankle. His little forehead wrinkled up as he stared at the makeshift brace. "How are rulers helping her stand up?"

Beckett sank down to the ground next to the boy. He was too tired to squat like the child was doing. He'd passed the age where a few hours of sleep on a tile floor was an acceptable night's rest. He explained how he'd made a brace to help stabilize Jess's ankle as he ate a muffin. His mom could chastise him for talking while eating another time.

"He reminds me of you as a child," his mom said quietly. "Always curious about everything. You had so many questions. Those questions would spawn more questions. You couldn't accept *I don't know* as an answer either. And it wasn't as if I could simply google it then. You drove me batty some days."

"That's definitely Mason." Jess smoothed the boy's blond locks and sighed. "Curious from dawn to dusk."

Beckett looked up at her. She had a grim set to her jaw, but he could see she was trying to put a smile on. Probably for Mason's benefit. She needed to get off that ankle and get a proper brace on it, most likely a cast.

"Mom, did you drive here?"

His mom looked confused at the sudden change of topic. "No, dear, your father dropped me off. Why?"

"Because we're heading to the hospital now and I don't want to leave you if you need a ride."

"Beckett—"

"Jessamine," he replied back evenly. "You need an X-ray. You have no car. Unless you want to get in the back of one of these understaffed ambulances, you are going to let me take you to the hospital."

They had a bit of a stare off, but finally she sighed. "Bring your truck over here. I don't think I can walk around that building again."

"You didn't walk around it the first time," Mason said with the bluntness of a child.

Beckett tried to keep his lips from curling up into a smile. He really did. But then Jess gave Mason a look of pure frustration and the chuckle he'd tried to choke back escaped. "He's not wrong," Beckett finally managed to get out around his peals of laughter.

"Hush, you." She wagged a finger at him. But he could see that she wasn't offended by their teasing. "Both of you. I don't see either one of you walking around with rulers and a stranger's sweater tied to your leg."

Moving swiftly, Beckett swooped her into his arms again. "You two ready to go?"

If his mother was surprised by his actions, she didn't show it. Jess gave a token protest, but then settled into his arms. He was a little surprised when she didn't fight him. He'd expected her to insist that he just bring the truck around, but she didn't. She must be in more pain than she was willing to let on.

Leaning in close, he whispered, "On a scale of one to ten, how bad is the pain?"

She murmured, "About a fifteen."

"That's what I thought." He didn't slow his pace until they reached his truck. He set her gently down on her uninjured ankle so that he could fish the keys out of his pocket. He unlocked the doors and had her installed in the front seat before she could issue a complaint.

"You should let your mother sit up front," she said as he slid behind the wheel.

"She'll be okay back there for the short trip to the hospital," he said. "Won't you, Mom?"

"Of course, dear." His mother's reply was swift and confident. She wouldn't take offense to Jess being up front, especially given her injuries, and if she had been offended, she was polite enough to address the slight in private later. "I'm content back here with this sweet child."

Jess tensed up.

"You okay?"

"Just a sharp pain," she said. But he wasn't quite sure he believed that was the cause of her tension. Still, he let the subject drop for the moment.

Mason was all too happy to keep the truck cab from lapsing into silence. He regaled them with a play-by-play. Surviving a tornado and being nearly buried alive was for certain an adventure to a small boy—one that he'd be proud to tell for the rest of his life, if Beckett was any judge. The child was quite animated as he told his story sitting next to Beckett's mother in the backseat. He soaked up her attention like a sponge, beaming at her whenever she made the appropriately awed sounds.

When he looked in the rearview mirror, Beckett could see the longing in his mother's eyes when she gazed at the little boy. He hadn't realized just how much she wanted to be a grandmother until that moment. She'd pushed for years, introducing him to women, suggesting how he might meet others, but it had never really occurred to him how much it truly meant to her.

He reached over and took Jess's hand. Stepkids had never been something he'd really considered one way or another until extremely recently. Seeing his mom with Mason though made him think that she wouldn't mind so much if her first grandkid wasn't a biological one. His dad might have other ideas, but he'd get over it.

Beckett rubbed his thumb against the back of Jess's hand. Would she even consider him as a potential stepdad for Mason? The idea was growing on him. Being with Jess meant that one of them had to move though. Woodvale's job market was hardly booming, and he'd established himself in Lexington. They'd been through a lot this past day together, and they'd certainly gotten a lot closer. But was that just from the stress they'd shared? Had she leaned on him for support because of her fear? And now that Mason was safe, would she push him away again?

CHAPTER TWENTY-THREE

GLANCING INTO THE BACKSEAT, Jess had to fight off a wince. Mason was engaged and clearly bonding with Mrs. Wilder, and she appeared enthralled with him. Great. Now there was a second person who had the power to break her little boy's heart. That was exactly what she'd feared might happen if she got involved with Beckett. She should have pushed him away. Sent him back when he had followed her into the school yesterday.

The best thing she could do would be to shut off all contact with Beckett. Keep her son far, far away from the Wilder family and anyone else who could hurt her son. The older woman ran her hand over Mason's hair and Jess had to blink back tears. How could she believe that someone so gentle might hurt her son? But it wasn't a physical hurt that she worried about now, was it? No, it was something far worse. Emotional pain could linger for years. She wanted to protect her son from that.

Beckett's thumb rubbed a tantalizing pattern against the top of her hand. Every brush of his skin against hers made her second-guess putting distance between them. Distance would mean no more of these loving, supportive touches. No more firm chest to rest her weary head on. No more strong arms to hold her when she felt weak.

Biting her lip, she stared down at their entwined hands. How had she let it get this far? There was no way to end this now without getting hurt. Even if she ended this as soon as she got to the hospital, she was already too attached. And so was Mason.

Tears filled her eyes and she fought valiantly to blink them away before anyone could see. Even if her heart was breaking at the thought of never being in Beckett's arms again, she had to do what was best for her little boy. She sniffled once. Oh, how she'd love to be selfish, to give herself over to Beckett's attention and let him love her. Mason's safety came first.

She shifted and pain shot up her ankle. Her grip on Beckett's hand tightened. Even while she was convincing herself to walk away from him and all that he had to offer, she was seeking his comfort. What had happened to her?

She'd been a strong, independent single mom two days ago.

I fell in love.

She looked over at him when that thought sank in. She'd done the stupid thing and gone and fallen for him. She really had. Closing her eyes, she let her mind consider all the paths forward. There was no way out of this where she didn't get hurt now. The best thing she could do was reject Beckett before he became attached to her. At least that way she could protect him from the heartbreak of losing a loved one.

Beckett pulled the truck to a stop in front of the main lobby of the hospital where there were crews putting up giant sheets of glass to replace the ones that had been shattered in the storm. "I'll need to go park the truck. But I figured you didn't want to walk from the parking garage or have me carry you that far."

He came around and helped her to the ground. "You good? I can take you inside and find a wheelchair or something."

She glared at him. Just because she had a bum leg didn't mean she was ready to accept a wheelchair. Determined to retain some measure of her independence, and to prove to herself that she could do without Beckett's assistance for a moment, she stood up as straight as she could. Her tone was firm, assertive, when she said, "I'll make it."

"I'm sure you will." Beckett just smiled at her, like he knew what she was thinking. Annoying man probably did. He'd known the whole time they were together, so it shouldn't surprise her that he did now.

"Go park your truck," she growled out at him.

"Yes, ma'am." He ruffled Mason's hair and told him, "Take care of your mother while I'm gone."

"You're going to the parking garage, not to war," Jess grumbled.

He laughed as he walked around the truck. "Falling in love is the biggest war there is."

And with that, he got in the cab and drove away.

"He... I... Ugh!" Jess shook her head. How infuriating! And to think just minutes ago she'd fancied herself in love with him!

"Mommy, I like him. Can we keep him?"

Jess opened her mouth and closed it again without speaking. She wasn't quite sure how to answer Mason's innocent query without shattering his hopes.

"While your mama does her goldfish impression, I'll tell you what you want to know." Jess bit the inside of her lip, hoping that Mrs. Wilder wasn't going to be rude. "You cannot simply keep people like they are stray puppies, but if you're lucky, they decide to stay of their own accord."

"Okay." Mason's lower lip popped out and he looked for a second like he might cry. But he quickly rallied. "He said he likes baseball. You think he would play with me?"

Mrs. Wilder answered with a smile that crinkled up her eyes just like Beckett's smile did his. "He more than likes baseball. He loves it. He was quite good when he used to play too. I'm sure if you ask nicely, and your mommy says it's okay, Beckett would love to take you to a game or maybe play catch."

"Yay!"

Great. Now Mason would for sure be heartbroken when she broke things off with Beckett. She took a step toward the hospital entrance too quickly, and in her haste, the injured ankle nearly gave way.

Mrs. Wilder caught her arm, helping her find her balance. She met Jess's eyes with a kind, steady look. They didn't share the same eye color, but there was something about her gaze that reminded Jess of Beckett. "Let's get you off that foot before you do further damage. Do you need to lean on me as we go in?"

Jess shook her head, reluctant to take help. As she slowly made her way inside, Mrs. Wilder hovered at her elbow, ready to steady her again if she were to wobble. She swallowed down the notion that she'd misjudged Mrs. Wilder just as she had Beckett.

"Thank you," she murmured when they reached the temporary check-in desk.

"Hey, Jess," Becky at the desk said. "Whatever have you done to yourself?"

"Broken or badly sprained this ankle. I could use an X-ray to be sure."

"Sure, sure." Becky tapped a few keys. "Are you up to date in the system?"

Jess nodded. She'd had to update all their info when Mason had needed stitches a couple months back. "Yeah, nothing has changed."

"Okay, I'll get you called back as soon as we can. It's a madhouse around here." She waved a hand at the cluster of chairs along the side wall. Most of them looked to be filled with people suffering various degrees of injury. "Take a seat…if you can find one."

She hobbled over to the seating area. Mrs. Wilder had found two seats together and there happened to be two across from them that were also unoccupied. Mason sat next to Mrs. Wilder, jabbering on happily to the older woman. Jess sank into one of the open seats, in too much pain to put an end to the obvious bonding her son and Beckett's mother were doing. "Dare I ask how y'all managed to find us seats together in this craziness?"

"If I know my mother, she gave someone a look until they decided they didn't need to be at the hospital any longer," Beckett joked as he sat next to her. "You get checked in?"

She nodded at him.

"Okay, good." He slipped an arm around her. "These chairs always seemed so uncomfortable before. It's amazing how spending a night on cold tile can change your perspective, huh?"

He'd changed his shirt while he was parking. Gone was the dirty, sweaty scrub top. He'd replaced it with a T-shirt advertising a local gym. And he had freshened up a little and now smelled like deodorant, rather than sweat and wet insulation.

"That shirt looks silly with those fancy pants," she teased.

"You know you like my fancy pants." He leaned over and brushed his lips across her forehead.

Jess tried to look at his mom and Mason, hoping they hadn't noticed Beckett's display of affection. That was too much to hope for. Mason and Mrs. Wilder were both grinning from ear to ear. Jess looked down. This was all too much. The longer she let this go on, the more people were at risk of getting hurt. She just didn't know how to put an end to it without seeming like a rude, ungrateful cow.

They all sat quietly until Jess was called. Mrs. Wilder offered to watch Mason while she saw the doctor, and Jess reluctantly agreed. Beckett stood and moved to go with her.

"I don't need a chaperone," she said softly.

"Maybe not." He followed along at her side, sharing her weight so that she could put less pressure on the foot. "But right now, you do need someone to lean on."

She didn't have the willpower to turn him back. If he wanted to offer his support, she'd accept it. At least for a little while longer. But soon, she'd have to step up and tell him that they could never be more than friends.

But she knew, deep in her heart, that she could never just be Beckett's friend. It would have to be all or nothing. If the day had taught her anything, it was that she couldn't resist Beckett—not his touch, or his words or the silent support his mere presence provided. One day in the very near future, she'd have to find a way to make that break. Before she got so attached to his presence that she couldn't.

She wasn't able to accept that maybe she was already too far gone to ever send him away. There was far too much at stake.

"This way, Jess," one of the newer nurses said, leading her down the hall to Radiology.

With Beckett's makeshift splint removed, Jess could see the swelling and the purple color tinging her skin. Even before the X-ray was snapped, she knew it was broken. Each time she'd shifted during the night, the jabs of pain had told her that she'd fractured the bone, but there'd been the tiniest sliver of hope that it wasn't. That hope vanished faster than candy with Mason's baseball team.

They put her in a curtained-off area to wait for the doctor.

Beckett sat next to her. "What color cast do you want?"

"You think it's broken too, don't you?"

"Afraid so."

She leaned her head back against the wall and stared up at the ceiling. "This is not the best time for this."

He pulled her hand into his lap and threaded their fingers together. "Honey, I don't think there's ever a good time for a broken ankle."

"Do you realize that I'm effectively home-less? My job is sorta rocky, considering the state of the emergency room. And I have a very active son to keep up with. Crutches just ain't gonna cut it."

"Your accent gets thicker when you're upset."

Jess let out a deep sigh. She worked hard to minimize her slow Southern drawl, but in times of stress, those old speech patterns came back to haunt her. "I'd tell you to hush up, but I'm too tired."

Dr. Newton came up just then. "So, it's definitely broken. The good news is that it's not surgical."

"And the bad news?"

"You're going to be rocking a cast for about six weeks. Longer if you don't stay off it and let your body recuperate." Dr. Newton paused and then gave Jess a knowing look. "Let's just go ahead and say you'll have the cast for eight weeks."

Beckett shook next to her with the effort of suppressing a laugh. "Sounds like she knows you, Jess."

"Now, no husbands or boyfriends are allowed where we're going, so I'm afraid I'll need to ask you to wait in the lobby." Dr. Newton flashed Beckett an apologetic smile. "We need to set the break and get her casted. Give us about two hours, give or take."

Beckett leaned over and brushed the softest of kisses against her lips. "I'll make sure Mason gets some food that's not sugary muffins, and maybe a nap. Call me when you're done?"

Once he'd walked away, Dr. Newton helped Jess into a wheelchair and pushed her up to the orthopedics unit. "I've seen him around the hospital. You are one lucky lady to go home to him every night."

Jess ignored that comment. Or tried to, anyway. "Do you think there's any chance at all that I could get a quick shower and a clean pair of scrubs before I get this cast on? I'm filthy."

Dr. Newton grunted. "I'll see what we can do."

It was a big ask, but if she didn't get a shower soon, she might lose her mind. And she did not want her sweaty, dirty leg casted where it would itch for weeks from the start.

Dr. Newton put her in a room. "We'll have to see if we can find someone to help you shower, unless you want to call your boyfriend back up?"

Jess shook her head quickly. "Could we call Freya Anderson? She's my best friend. Maybe if she's not too busy, she wouldn't mind helping me."

Freya, of course, came when she was called and had a clean set of scrubs in her hands. Shaking her head, she looked down at Jess with worry filling her eyes. "Tell me how badly I need to hurt him?"

"Who?"

"Beckett!" she exclaimed. "He was supposed to watch out for you, not let you break a leg. I suppose I should be glad that you didn't break your frickin' neck!"

"This is all on me." Jess shrugged. "I did that impulsive thing where I think I know better than the person in charge and rushed in without a plan. This is where it got me."

"He still promised me that he'd stay with you."

"Oh, so you're the reason he's been babysitting me?" Jess winced as Freya helped her to her feet and into the shower. Freya helped her undress and stood outside the curtain while Jess quickly washed the muck and grime from her skin.

As the water poured over her, she tried to wash away the hurt feelings that Freya's words manifested. How much of Beckett's attentiveness had been because he wanted to be with her and how much of it came from a promise made to Freya?

"I know what you're thinking," Freya said loudly enough to be heard over the water. "Jess, if you think for one second that man didn't stay with you of his own accord, you are blind. I just wanted to make sure he didn't let you run off alone. You needed someone with you, in case—"

"In case Mason had been hurt, or worse," Jess finished for her.

"But since you're here alone, the jerk did leave you. He promised me he wouldn't."

Jess pulled the curtain back so that she could see Freya's face. "He's down in the lobby with his mom and Mason."

"Oh, is he now?" Freya's mood brightened considerably. "Is that why you were so anxious for a shower that you paged me away from the chaos I've been dealing with to help you clean up?"

"Maybe I was tired of smelling myself." Jess tugged the curtain closed and dried herself off as best she could without putting any weight on her foot.

Freya had to help her get the clean scrub pants on. "Oh, come on. That man is hot. Girl, I saw you noticing him. You can't lie to me." Freya raised a brow and stared Jess down.

"Yes, I noticed that he's attractive. I'm celibate, not dead." Jess didn't like the calculating look Freya gave her. It didn't bode well.

"Jess…"

"Freya, just leave it alone. Please? I'm single and happy that way." And she could nurse her achy heart in peace without her best friend's fussing if she didn't tell Freya about how close she was to changing her opinion on being single.

"Are you sure?" Freya's eyes sparkled. "Oh, wait, I forgot who I was talking to for a minute. You know there is more to life than this job and your son, right? Let your hair down on occasion. Have a little fun. Spending some, shall we say, adult time, with a man might do you a world of good. Especially with a guy who looks like Beckett Wilder. Just think about it."

Freya left her with that and went back to work. Just think about it. As if Jess hadn't been doing just that... She could think of nothing else. Her work was a mess, her house was un-livable and she had a broken bone. Did any of those things jump to the forefront of her mind? Nope. All she could think about was Beckett Wilder and the way her heart sped up when he smiled at her.

Jess toughed her way through the bone reset with only minimal pain medication. She didn't want her head to get too foggy when she had Mason with her to think about. But she also knew better than to try to do it with zero medi-cation.

Once the bone was set, they slipped a stock-inette over her foot gently and started wrap-ping it with thick padding. Once they had the padding spread so that there was even pressure around her foot and ankle, they showed her the fiberglass casting options. She really didn't care what color her cast was, but she settled on the purple since it was her favorite color.

The technician worked quickly, wrapping the damp material around her foot and ankle, over the padding. The fiberglass casting was lighter weight than the traditional plaster and allowed better airflow.

"Am I getting fiberglass because Dr. Newton wants more X-rays soon?"

"Yes, ma'am." The technician stood and washed her hands. "This will take at least thirty minutes to harden enough for us to let you out of here. But it should be completely dry in about two hours. When I come back in to check that it's dry, I'll bring your care instructions. Don't touch it while I'm gone."

CHAPTER TWENTY-FOUR

WHEN BECKETT GOT BACK to the lobby, his dad stood in front of his mom's chair. His shoulders drooped with visible exhaustion. How long had he been on his feet?

Mason had fallen asleep. His head rested in Beckett's mom's lap. His mouth gaped open in sleep, and he was the picture of pure innocence.

They all looked worn out.

"Beckett," his mom said with a warm smile when he walked up. "How's she doing?"

"Broken ankle, as I expected. She's getting a cast now. They said it would be a couple hours before she was ready to go." He smoothed a stray lock of hair out of Mason's face, taking care not to wake him. "Forgive me for saying this, but you all look exhausted. Mason is clearly worn out. Would you consider taking Mason home with you and getting some rest?"

"Is Jess okay with that?" his mom questioned.

"I think she'll be upset, but I'll take the

blame." He didn't just *think* she'd be upset. He knew it for a fact. But Mason was exhausted, and he couldn't sleep in these chairs. Not to mention, they had nowhere else to go really. He'd take whatever Jess had to say with the knowledge that he'd done what he thought was best at the time.

"We'll take him home with us, but you be sure you tell her that he's okay. She'll worry."

"Got it." He bent and lifted Mason easily into his arms. The boy shifted, and murmured something, but thankfully didn't wake. "I'll help get him to the car."

When his dad cleared his throat, Beckett paused. Maybe he should have cleared this plan with his parents first since he was commandeering their house, but it wasn't like there was another real option. "If that's okay with you?"

His dad nodded slowly. "Of course."

With that settled, he helped them out to his father's car, settling Mason in the backseat. Hopefully, they could get the boy in the house without too much trouble. His father didn't need to be lifting Mason's weight with his chemo port.

His dad waited until his mom had gotten in the car too before he spoke. "The boy's mother, she means something to you?"

Beckett nodded. It was a little early to be professing his love, but he definitely had caught feelings for Jess. Strong ones. And he found himself already feeling protective of Mason. It was a lot to communicate in a nod, but his dad interpreted the message without issue.

"I'll make sure he's safe then. We'll see you soon."

Beckett breathed a sigh of relief when his dad drove away with Mason. He and the man had certainly had their issues over the years, mostly in regard to Beckett's career, but his father was a man of his word. Beckett knew without a doubt that his dad would take them straight home where his mother would then fuss over Mason like he was royalty. And with them all safe, he could devote his full attention to Jess.

He went back into the hospital lobby to wait. After managing to snag a chair in the corner, Beckett closed his eyes to rest a moment while he waited for Jess. He needed sleep, a shower and a sandwich and he wasn't even picky about the order he got them in. He must have drifted off, because the next thing he knew, Jess was in front of him in a wheelchair poking his knee.

"Where's my son?"

Beckett sat up straight and blinked at her for a moment while he tried to clear his sleep-addled mind. "He's at my parents' house."

"Excuse me?"

"He was exhausted. My parents were both dead on their feet. I thought they'd all be more comfortable at my parents' house." He hoped that would take away some of the ire he read in her expression. His mom had been right about Jess's reaction. But this icy anger was a little scarier than the fiery temper she'd shown before.

"I'd really like to get my son and go home."

"I'll get my truck." He stood and moved around her without touching her. The ice queen was back, and he wanted to give her a moment to thaw before he reminded her that her home had been destroyed by the tornado.

Soon he had her in the cab of the truck and headed away from the hospital. They'd gone about three blocks when she said, "Did your parents move? I thought you grew up on the lake."

"No."

He pulled into the drive of her damaged home. "I'm not trying to hurt you here but look at your house. Honey, you can't stay here. You can't go home. You're pissed at me, aren't you? But your son was asleep in one of those miserable waiting room chairs. Which he almost fell out of, by the way. So, I made a judgment call. I chose to send him home with my parents where he would be safe, looked after and could rest in a proper bed."

"You should have asked me first," she said quietly.

"Where you'd have protested that you'd rather go to a hotel. Look around. With the widespread devastation in Woodvale and the surrounding communities, there won't be a hotel room for miles. My parents have the space."

"You still should have asked me."

"I did what I thought was right. I won't apologize for it."

Beckett backed out of the drive, and they drove the rest of the way to his parents' house in silence. He'd done nothing wrong. How could she be mad at him for taking care of her son when she wasn't able to?

They were still not speaking when he parked his truck by the front steps. "I'll have to carry you in, but we have a set of crutches in the attic. I'll get them down for you so that you can have some freedom back."

"Thank you."

He expected her to hold herself stiffly in his arms, reluctant to accept his touch, but she wrapped her arms around his neck and leaned into his shoulder. "You are driving me crazy, woman," he told her as he carried her over the threshold.

"Ditto."

"The guest rooms are just over here," he told

her as they passed the open living room and kitchen. He didn't see his parents or Mason. They must all be resting. "There are two guest rooms on the left that share a bath, and my room is on the right."

"I just want to see Mason," she said.

He eased her down at the doorway to the first guest room. It wasn't shut completely. Peering through the crack, Beckett saw Mason curled up asleep wearing one of his T-shirts. He looked as though he'd had a bath.

"Mommy?" Mason said sleepily.

"Hey, baby," she said, holding on to the door frame for balance. "I didn't mean to wake you up."

"If you're good here, I'll go find those crutches for you," Beckett offered.

"Thanks."

It took him a few minutes to find the crutches. His mom tended to be a pack rat and she wanted to keep everything because she might use it someday. When he came back down, he paused when he heard a snippet of conversation that set his mind churning.

"Mommy, I like it here."

"You do?" Jess responded. "I'm happy that you like it, but…" Beckett heard her sigh.

"It kinda made me miss Nana though. I wish I still had a nana or a grandma or grandpa."

Beckett dared to peek around the doorway. "Since you kissed Mr. Wilder, does that mean he's going to be my dad now?"

"Honey, it's not that simple."

"Grown-ups make everything hard."

He didn't want to be accused of eavesdropping, and he sure didn't want to tell her what he'd just overheard, so he backed up quietly and then made more noise than usual when he walked up to the bedroom again. Mason wanted him to be his dad? The first time Mason had said it Beckett had been amused, but it was different this time, because now Beckett had feelings for Mason's mom and becoming his dad was a real possibility. A shard of fear lodged itself in Beckett's heart.

He tapped on the open door. "I found those crutches. I'll be across the hall if you need anything."

After going into his room, he closed the door and leaned against the cool wood. Thoughts spun through his brain, powered by a tornado of emotions. The last day and a half had given him a lot to process. Most importantly, was he really dad material?

CHAPTER TWENTY-FIVE

AFTER BECKETT HAD said goodnight, Mason had settled back down relatively quickly and dozed off, leaving Jess with far too much time to think. Physically, she was exhausted, but her mind kept going over the conversation with Mason she was sure Beckett had overheard. He had a look in his eyes, sort of a panicked confusion. If she wasn't mistaken, that was the moment it had really hit him that she came as a package deal with a son.

Twice, she got the crutches and went to the door, but she chickened out before she could go talk to him. They had no future, and she knew that, but she needed one more night with the illusion that things were different. She had finally calmed enough that she was dozing lightly when she heard Beckett and his dad talking.

Hearing her name brought her back to being fully awake.

"If your plans haven't changed, then why

would you get involved with her, son?" His dad didn't make much effort to keep his voice down. "Her life is here, and yours is in Lexington."

"She could come with me."

"Have you talked to her about that?"

Beckett's silence was answer enough. The conversation trailed off, leaving Jess with even more to think about. Beckett had told her that he would think about staying in Woodvale, hadn't he? She wracked her brain trying to remember the exact words he'd used, but she was too tired to clearly recall.

Still, sleep was a long time coming. When she did finally nod off, her slumber was restless and filled with dreams of Beckett leaving them and breaking Mason's heart.

When she woke at five, she gave in to the impulse to talk to Beckett. She had to find out how he felt, and what he planned to do, so that she could figure out how to move forward. Tapping lightly on his door, she waited for him to answer.

"Is something wrong?" Beckett opened the door wearing nothing but a pair of low-slung athletic shorts. He rubbed the sleep from his eyes, the movements causing the muscles in his arms to ripple intriguingly.

"We need to talk."

"Talk?" Beckett pulled her into his arms. "I'm all for a private conversation."

His mouth scorched hot against hers. Her arms came up around his neck and she leaned into his embrace. Her crutches fell to the carpeted floor with a muffled clatter.

Not what she came for, but she enjoyed his attentions for a moment before reluctantly pushing him away. "I meant really talk," she said as she tried to catch her breath.

"Okay, we can talk." He pushed the door closed behind her.

"I overheard part of your conversation with your dad." She waited for him to say something, to deny that he was still planning to leave. There was still the tiniest sliver of hope in her heart, but his silence squashed that. She swallowed hard and put a hand on his chest to push him back, to put some distance between them so that she could think. "You are still planning to leave, after all that you said."

"I have a career in Lexington." He tried to move closer. "You and Mason could come with me."

"No," she whispered. "My life is here. Mason's life is here."

"We can make a new life, together," he argued, his hands clutching at her waist. "Won't you at least consider it?"

She shook her head, as angry with herself as she was at him. She'd let her guard down with him, and that part was entirely on her. Still, he'd told her that he would consider staying in Wood-vale. And that simple fact had been part of why she'd let him get so close. "I knew I shouldn't get involved with you. I knew that letting you near Mason was a bad idea. The day we met, I warned you to keep your distance. And this is why."

"You were afraid I'd want to have a future with you?" he scoffed.

She choked back a sob. "I was afraid that you'd walk away and leave me just like Clint did. But now it's not just my heart on the line. It's Mason's too."

"I'm not Clint," he growled out through clenched teeth. "It doesn't have to be that way."

"I know that." She wrapped her arms around herself, trying to give herself the strength to get through this conversation. "But I totally called this one, didn't I?"

"You assume that I'd, what? Knock you up and bail? Hurt your son?" He shook his head. "Is that really what you think of me?"

"I didn't think Clint would hurt me either." She snorted. "Then I found out that the man I was in love with wasn't who he said he was.

He was my everything, and to him I was just a sidepiece. I lost my boyfriend, my pride and my reputation in a single blow. Now I have Mason to think of."

"You think I'd hurt Mason." Pain layered over his words, and she clenched her hands against his chest.

"Maybe not intentionally," she had to admit. "But when you go back to Lexington, he's going to be hurt. Even if this morning is the last time that you see him, he will still be hurt that he doesn't get to hang out with you again. He's crazy about you already."

"So you're pushing me away because me leaving will hurt Mason?" He huffed. "You know that doesn't make sense."

"You are the one leaving town! I'm not pushing you away—you're doing that all on your own." Tears welled up in her eyes and she swiped roughly at them. "This is why I didn't want to get involved with you!" Fat tears ran down her cheeks. "I knew it could only end in tears. But you had to be so...you."

"So me?" he said with a hint of a smile. "Is that an insult or a compliment?"

"Why did you have to be so caring? So supportive? If you'd been even half the jerk that Clint was, I could have walked away without giving you a second glance. But no, you had to be this perfect package. All good-looking and kind and taking charge without being a jerk about it. You had to go and make me…"

"Make you what, Jess?" Beckett moved closer, slowly like a predator easing up on his prey. "Make you like me?" With the barest of touches, he let his fingertips trail along her jawline. "Make you want me?" Barely a breath separated them when he whispered, "Make you love me?"

"I can't."

"But you already do, don't you?" His lips traced the curve of her throat. "What I'm feeling isn't one-sided here."

She couldn't stop her reactions to him any more than she could stop the sun from rising or rain from falling from the sky. "I can't," she argued, even as she clutched his shoulders in her hands and wished that things were different.

"You just have to let me in. You and Mason could move with me to Lexington when I go back." He held her so tenderly that she almost thought they could make something work. "I've got a job waiting for me there. You know there's no job market here for an EMT. But I'm sure you could find a job in Lexington easily, as a nurse or another management-type position."

He wanted her to give up everything for him. Put herself in a place of being totally dependent upon a man again. A position she'd sworn she'd never be in again.

"Woodvale is my home."

"What's keeping you here?" Tension tightened his frame. "Memories and a falling-down house? I'll buy us a house in Lexington."

"My dad grew up in that falling-down house, and so did I. If I have any say, Mason will grow up there too." That damaged house held so many memories. And memories were all that remained now of her mom and dad.

Frustration showed on his face. "So you're choosing a town that's done nothing but keep you down and a damaged house over me, because of what?"

"That damaged house is all I have left of my parents. I may not have much here, but I have Freya who is the closest thing I have to a sibling. And I have my job that I happen to like." Her heart was breaking even as the words slipped past her lips. "I can't go with you to Lexington."

"Won't."

"What?"

"You *can* go, you just won't."

"That's not fair. Woodvale is my home, and my son's safety and well-being has to be my top priority."

Beckett suddenly took a step back. He bent

and picked up her crutches. Ice laced his voice. "If you don't trust me with Mason, and you don't want a future with me, then I suppose there's nothing left to say. You're welcome to stay here until you can make alternate arrangements. I'll do my best not to burden you with my unwanted presence."

Jess shivered at the sudden coldness between them. She'd gotten what she wanted, hadn't she? She'd just been asking him to let her go, but she hadn't expected it to feel so wrong. "Beckett…"

"Do I need to leave, or can I have my room back?" He opened the door and kept his eyes trained on the floor.

"I'll go." She tucked the crutches under her arms. When she cleared the doorway, Beckett closed the door behind her. He didn't slam it, but the audible click of the closure carried a finality to it.

The moment she got back into her room, she used the landline on the table and called Freya. "It's early, but can you come get us?"

"Tell me where. Why do you sound like you've been crying?"

She gave Freya the address and a promise to explain later. She couldn't rehash the conversation with Beckett without bursting into tears, and she would be doing so with a heavy heart.

The best thing for Mason was for them to make a clean break from Beckett and the Wilders, wasn't it? So why did it feel like the worst thing for her?

CHAPTER TWENTY-SIX

THE HARDEST THING he'd ever had to do was put the woman he loved in a car and let her drive away. He rubbed at his chest, trying to ease the pain around his heart. Sinking down on the porch steps, Beckett tried to remember how to breathe.

He'd told her that he was falling for her, that he wanted a future with her, and she'd walked away. He'd been sure that she'd returned his sentiments, but still she hadn't stayed. The distance she put between them she claimed was to protect Mason, but it was all really to protect herself. Mason was completely safe with him, and she had to know that. No, this was because Jess didn't trust him. Or maybe didn't trust herself around him. Either way, she was gone.

"Want to get something off your chest, son?" His dad sat down beside him.

Beckett huffed. "Like what? That my future just drove away without me, determined to never let me out of the present because of a past I had nothing to do with?"

"You can't change the past." His father slapped him on the back. "But the good news is that the future is a little more malleable."

"I don't see how." He waved a hand toward the road. "Did you not see her drive away without a backward glance?"

"We haven't had the closest relationship, and I accept the bulk of the responsibility for that." His dad leaned back, stretching his legs out in front of him. "But I see how you look at Jess and her boy. Your mom is in love with that little guy already."

Beckett couldn't stop the rude reply that broached his lips. "All things I know, Dad."

"I'm going to let the disrespect in your tone slide this time because I know you're smarting at the loss of your lady. I won't sit here and be the target for your wrath though." His dad rose to his feet. "If you aren't going to do whatever you can to get her back, you'd better get that out of your system fast."

Beckett flashed his father an apologetic look.

His dad stopped him before Beckett could verbally acknowledge taking his frustrations out on him. "You want her back, right? Take care of her present needs, and the future will fall into line."

With those final words of wisdom, the man went back inside the house, leaving Beckett to think about the advice he'd been given. His dad seemed to think things with Jess could still be fixed. To Beckett, the future looked bleak. He didn't see a path forward that gave him a future with Jess. She didn't trust him, but once he thought about it more, it became clear that she was trying to consider Mason's best interests. How could he be mad about that?

Could his dad be right though?

Take care of her present needs.

What did she need most? And how could he provide that for her?

CHAPTER TWENTY-SEVEN

LOSING CLINT WHEN she was expecting Mason had hurt, but it was nothing compared to losing Beckett. Three days had passed since she'd walked away from him, her eyes filled with tears. It had taken her about an hour to realize that while she'd been infatuated with Clint, and at the time thought herself to be in love, it was Beckett who her heart truly desired.

She let out a deep sigh, filled with unrequited longing.

"If you miss him that much, why don't you call him?" Freya asked gently. They'd been staying with Freya since leaving the Wilders' home. The apartment was cramped. Even Mason had complained about the lack of space. Jess hadn't had the heart to argue about that, since she herself was sleeping on the couch. A very lumpy couch, at that.

The jab that really hurt though was when Mason had asked when they'd see Beckett again.

In only a few interactions, he'd taken to Beckett easily. Her little boy had fallen for Beckett just like she had, and she hadn't had it in her to crush his hopes yet. She'd put him off, saying Beckett was busy with the storm cleanup.

"It's not that simple." Jess stirred her coffee, playing with it rather than drinking it. She wanted to explain, but the words just weren't there. Her mind told her that being with Beckett was an unacceptable risk, but her heart wanted him with every beat it took. And because of that, there was no explanation that fully sat right.

"Bull." Freya set her coffee mug down on the table. She reached across and put her hand on top of Jess's. "You're in love with him. He's clearly crazy about you." She glanced toward the spare bedroom where Mason was still sleeping and lowered her voice to a whisper. "And you can't think that Mason would be upset if you and Beckett got together."

Jess didn't respond. It sounded so easy when Freya could put it in such straightforward terms. But Freya hadn't seen the hollowness in Beckett's eyes when he'd thrown her out of his room, or felt the change in his touch when he'd helped her down the stairs to Freya's car.

"Well, if you aren't going to do the right thing, I can't make you." Freya poured out the last of her coffee and stuck the mug in the dishwasher. "I have some things to do this afternoon, but you mentioned going by your house to see what we could salvage. You want to get Mason up and ready?"

Jess slowly got to her feet. She doubted there was much that could be saved from that damaged house. The only thing worse off in her life right now than that storm-ravaged house was her broken heart.

They did need to see what could be recovered though. Maybe some of their clothes could be washed and would be usable, but Jess feared that all of the furnishings would be a total loss. Mason had expressed hope that some of his toys had survived, so he would be eager to get up and go with them to see what he could find.

An hour later, Freya pulled up to the front of Jess's house. A construction crew had started putting up new roof trusses. Stacks of shingles and supplies sat next to the fence. Another group of people seemed to be carrying her belongings out of the house and sorting them into bins. It looked like a beehive with all the activity buzzing in and out.

"What in the world?" Jess murmured as she got out of the car. "Did you do this?" she asked Freya.

"No, but I was aware of it, and I've been in

contact with the man in charge," Freya said quietly. "Don't hate me too hard."

"Who then?" Jess made her way up the sidewalk slowly, taking care to balance on the uneven concrete walk. It had been on her list of things to fix, but after the tornado that list had grown exponentially, with the sidewalk slipping down near the bottom. "Where did all these people come from?"

As if in answer to her question, Beckett walked out the open front door. "We need to get the roof on quickly and—"

He stopped midsentence, his eyes greedily searching her face. She heated under his scrutiny, wishing she'd taken more care with her appearance.

The man he was talking to wore a hard hat and a T-shirt with the logo of a construction company on the front. "Roof is the top priority, of course, Mr. Wilder." As if sensing that he wouldn't get a reply from Beckett, he spoke quickly before walking away.

"Beckett!" Mason called from behind Jess. He rushed around her and flung himself into Beckett's legs. "I been asking Mommy when we could see you. She said you were busy, but she didn't tell me that you were busy here. Are you fixing our house? Was it supposed to be a surprise for me?"

"Was it a good surprise? I'd hoped to get it done before you found out." Tousling the boy's hair, Beckett answered him while keeping his gaze locked on Jess's. "As cool as lying in your bed looking at real stars might be, I couldn't let you and your mom have a house without a roof."

Mason, oblivious to the tension between the two adults, launched into a detailed description of the field trip his class had taken to the planetarium and all the things he knew about stars. Then he spotted a bunch of his things in one of the bins in the yard. He rushed over to check it out, leaving Beckett and Jess to awkwardly try to get through their first meeting since things went sideways.

Beckett gave her a grim smile. The normal lightness she associated with Beckett was missing from his eyes. Even when they'd argued, there'd been a happiness about him that had drawn her in. It was missing. Had her actions taken that from him?

"You didn't have to do this," she said quietly.

"A man takes care of his family." He gave that simple explanation with a shrug.

His family? Jess sucked in a sharp breath. Beckett considered them his family? That casual lift of his shoulders that implied everything he'd done here was no biggie frustrated her to no end. He brushed it off like he'd done virtually nothing, maybe brought them a pizza for dinner or something of little consequence. Providing them with a livable home was the biggest of deals in that moment, especially since he knew how much the house meant to her.

"Beckett, look what I found!" Mason squealed as he ran back up with a baseball and glove in his hand. "Can we play catch? Please!"

Beckett nodded and walked toward the backyard with Mason skipping along happily at his heels. When he looked over his shoulder at her, Jess nearly burst into tears.

Jess watched them go, her heart in her throat. He'd been the last person she'd expected.

Freya nudged her, almost tipping her over. "Weren't you going to go through your things?"

"Why would he do all this?" She waved a hand from the house to the yard and back. "He was so angry with me. He hasn't spoken to me in days."

"You really don't have a clue, do you?" Freya snickered. "Dang, girl, but you are blind if you don't see it."

Jess looked at her in confusion. "See what?"

"That my son is in love with you."

"Mr. Wilder!" Jess nearly tipped over as she spun to face Beckett's father. "I didn't see you there."

"Beckett's been insistent that we get this

house livable for you and Mason." Mr. Wilder gave her a scrutinizing gaze. "I don't know what you fought over. But if you feel the same way, you might want to tell him. That boy of mine is stubborn. If he thinks you don't want him, he's going to stay out of your way. This is as close to a declaration of love as you'll get from him if you don't give him a sign that his attention is wanted."

Jess gaped at him, completely unsure of what to say.

"I hope you'll excuse me. I have an appointment." He walked over to the fence and called out to Beckett, tapping his fingers on the face of his watch.

Beckett came out of the yard with Mason at his side. "I'll play catch with you another day, if your mom says it's okay. She has my number. Just tell her to give me a time."

He made eye contact with Jess. "All she has to do is call."

Her breath hung in her throat. He really was just waiting for her to invite him back into her life. She hadn't believed it. Even given his father's open speech and Freya's teasing jabs, Jess had been convinced she'd ruined things permanently with Beckett. Now she was less sure.

Still, nothing had changed really. Beckett still wanted to go back to Lexington while she was firmly rooted here. She'd have to give up so much—her career, her family home and her hometown and all the memories of her parents. Moving to Lexington would mean putting her faith in Beckett, trusting him to provide for both her and Mason until she could find a job.

Was what she and Beckett could have worth that risk?

As she watched Beckett and his dad drive away, another idea came to mind. It would take some coordinating, but it might be the only way for them both to truly get what they wanted.

CHAPTER TWENTY-EIGHT

JESS IMPATIENTLY STRAIGHTENED the files on her desk. It had taken her a solid week and a half to put the proposal together. She'd checked and triple-checked the numbers before reaching out. Even though she was as prepared as she could be for this meeting, her nerves were completely shot.

She looked up at the sharp single knock.

"May I come in?" Richard Wilder stood in the open doorway.

"Please," she said, waving for him to take the empty chair across from her desk. "Thank you for agreeing to meet with me today, Mr. Wilder."

"Richard, please."

She nodded. "I wanted to talk to you about the emergency department proposal before I submitted it."

His eyebrows rose and she swallowed hard at how much the man across from her reminded her of Beckett. "My son is handling all of the proposals. Now, I know you've had a falling out—"

"Will you at least look at it?" She bit her lip as she waited for his answer. "And I know the ambulance service here in Woodvale is a bone of contention between you and Beckett, so I didn't want to have this come as a surprise or exacerbate the issues between the two of you."

He motioned for her to continue.

After handing him the folder, she gave him a quick pitch. He said nothing in response. She'd expected a few questions. Maybe some arguments. But she didn't expect silence. Did he hate it? Nothing in his expression gave her a hint either way. As the minutes ticked past while he flipped through the printed proposal, she grew more and more anxious.

This was the best chance she had to fix things with Beckett. She didn't have a backup plan really. Maybe she should reiterate some of her key points?

"You've really thought this out," he finally said.

She breathed a sigh of relief. That wasn't an instant no. Good sign, right? "I tried to consider all the angles. Some of the data Beckett and I worked on together. Not in this form, but he helped me with determining needs during our meeting before the tornado. As you know, he has far more experience in that area than I do."

"You've sold me on the concept, but I'm not in charge of this project."

"I was hoping you could still help me out." She blurted out the rest of her plan, the part that had little to do with funding, and everything to do with love.

CHAPTER TWENTY-NINE

IT HAD BEEN three weeks since he'd last laid eyes on her. A busy period, thankfully, since it hadn't left him too much time to dwell on losing Jess. He hadn't initiated the fixing of her house as an excuse to bump into her, but he wasn't upset that he had run into her and Mason that day. He'd made it clear that the ball was in her court, hadn't he? She hadn't called though, and no matter how many times he looked at his phone, she hadn't texted either. So, what could he do but assume she had no interest in seeing him?

Beckett got to the hospital about thirty minutes before the monthly special committee meeting was due to begin. He had received all the proposals and was set to make some announcements which he considered a top priority. To his frustration, his father had stepped in and taken over the proposal and funding for the emergency department. Beckett wasn't sure if it was to take away the opportunity for him to fund the ambulances or to limit his contact with Jess.

He sat with his head in his hands trying to find a way to address the committee without making a fool of himself. It would seem rude if he avoided Jess but making eye contact might make him lose his train of thought. Every time she crossed his mind, he got distracted by the what-ifs and what-could-have-beens.

Lasting relationships had never been his strong suit. In the past though, his job had always played a role in ending things for him. Sometimes women romanticized dating a first responder, loving the idea of a man in uniform more than the actual reality. Things would be great for a few weeks, until she wanted to take a trip away only to realize he worked nearly every weekend. His odd hours would inevitably begin to chafe, and he'd never had a strong enough connection with a woman to fight past the schedule frustrations.

Until Jess...

Now his schedule wasn't the issue, but the location of his job. He'd have to give up being an EMT permanently if he moved here. Even with the requested budget that he and Jess had worked up, there wouldn't be much for him. The only EMT position open was on third shift, and he'd never see her and Mason. Still, he'd filled out the application and it was on hold waiting for him to click Submit.

When people started filing into the room, Beckett didn't look up. Even still, he knew the exact moment Jess walked through the door. She hadn't spoken, but he was aware of her arrival, nonetheless. He took a deep breath. This would be so much easier if she didn't want to be with him at all.

Being together should be easy. Love shouldn't mean choosing between your partner and your career though.

"Okay, looks like everyone is here." Freya kicked the meeting off. Beckett risked looking up at her as she filled everyone in on the current status of repairs to the emergency department and the estimated timeline to completion. She gave a brief rundown of exactly what their insurance was covering and how that affected the budget.

"Now, I think Beckett has some announcements to make regarding the funding his family's foundation is graciously donating." Freya gestured, indicating for him to begin when ready.

He took a deep breath. Eventually, public speaking had to get easier. While he'd never have his dad's eloquence in front of a crowd, he hoped he at least wouldn't get so flustered that he looked like an idiot.

Jess cleared her throat.

He glanced her way, looking down at the table before he could meet her gaze. Not looking at her took far more effort than he'd anticipated. "Do you have a concern before I get to the numbers?"

"I do, actually." He heard her chair squeak as she stood up. "We need more EMT funding, and we need it now."

Jerking his gaze up to her face, he stared at her in shock. His forehead wrinkled in confusion. Had he hallucinated? He waited for her to continue, sure that there had to be a catch or that she was about to completely contradict what she'd just said. She'd argued from the get-go that her emergency department came first, although she'd acknowledged that more ambulances were needed. And they'd come to the conclusion together that there would be no way to fund more ambulances unless they had more outside income.

"The problem I see is that this is beyond the scope of what should fit into the budget of the emergency department. I've submitted a proposal for an all new department—call it the Department for Emergency Services for now, if you will. Ambulances and EMTs are outside the bounds of what should be considered as part of the ED. They need their own department, with a leader willing to advocate for his team's needs, no longer stuffed under the umbrella of the emergency department where they have to fight for funding against trauma surgeons and strep tests."

The room was quiet as the committee seemed to digest Jess's words. Beckett couldn't blame them for needing a moment. He was a little dumbfounded himself. Not only was she agreeing with him, she'd taken his plans and supersized them.

"Would you be in charge of this new department as well?" someone asked.

"No, not at all. I am not the ideal person for that role." Her lips upturned when she looked at him. That soft, shy smile made him sure that it would be ten times harder to move on than he'd imagined it would be. "But I think Beckett Wilder would do an admirable job as the head of the new department. Don't you?"

"Any opposed to giving this idea further merit?" Freya asked.

Beckett's dad stood and cleared his throat. "Jess has shown me her proposal. It needs a little more work, but I think we can make something happen. And Beckett's welcome to apply for the position, but he'll have to earn it fairly."

Beckett sank into his chair. His mind was a million miles from where it should be, focusing on where Jess had taken this meeting instead of where it was meant to go. If this went through, it would accomplish all that he'd been shooting for here in Woodvale. He'd fought so hard for it that he didn't know what to do with himself now that the issue was on its way to resolution and even his father seemed to be on board.

His dad placed a hand on his shoulder. "Do you think you could help Jess get that proposal cleaned up? She doesn't have the experience that you have with running an ambulance. I think you'd have a better idea of whether or not the proposed budget is viable."

He nodded slowly. Oh, man, getting that proposal together would mean working alone side by side to get it complete and ready to submit. Could she stand to be in his presence that long? More importantly, could he make it through even an hour alone with her without taking her in his arms and giving her a physical reminder of just how good they could be together?

He scrubbed a hand over his face and pondered the woman across from him. It was through her that his wishes were finally becoming reality, at least when it came to the hospital and their hometown. If only she'd make such an about-face when it came to a relationship with him, then all of his dreams would come true. When he looked up, their eyes met and there was a hint of something in her gaze that made it hard to breathe.

He sat up a little straighter and had to bite the inside of his cheek to stop himself from blurting out how much he missed her in front of all the members of the special committee. She'd captured his heart the way no other woman ever had and nearly broken him when she sent him away. The longing in her eyes sent a spark of awareness coursing through him.

She'd changed her opinion on EMT funding. Dare he hope she'd reconsidered their relationship?

CHAPTER THIRTY

BUTTERFLIES FLUTTERED IN Jess's stomach as the others filed out of the conference room. No, they were too big to be butterflies. More like pterodactyls. She took a deep breath and tried to quell her ragged nerves.

Beckett had made the first move when he had worked so hard to get her house ready to be lived in. He hadn't sought credit for his acts, and if she hadn't caught him, he'd probably have let her think it was a guardian angel who wanted to remain anonymous.

Freya was the last one to leave the room, and she gave Jess's arm a reassuring squeeze. "Get your man back," she whispered.

"So," she began. Briefly, she'd considered simply throwing herself into his arms, thinking he'd certainly see that as an apology. That wouldn't be fair though. She owed him an earnest apology and a verbal declaration of her love.

"So," he repeated when she didn't say anything besides that single syllable. "Thank you for finally seeing the merit in my idea. I appreciate your vote of confidence in recommending me to lead the new department too. If you want to let me know when a convenient time to work on the proposal would be, I'll make the timing work."

His words caused an ache deep in her chest. He hadn't completely dismissed her, but she'd held out hope that he might be a little more pleased. She had only herself to blame for Beckett's current attitude though. She'd hurt him. Maybe one day she could tell him about how badly she'd hurt her own stubborn self too.

"If you had been anyone else, life would be so simple." She winced as the words came out of her mouth. That was not what she meant to say at all. She'd rehearsed a speech, a true apology. She'd made enough mistakes with this man. She didn't need to make more with impetuous words.

"Am I supposed to apologize for being myself?" He pinched the bridge of his nose. "I can't change who I am, even if you want me to. We aren't talking about how my job frustrates you or how you might want me to break an annoying habit. The part of me you object to isn't something within my power to change."

"I don't want you to change. Well, other than

your address. I really would like to stay here in Woodvale." She smiled sadly at him as she moved over to take the seat next to his. "I fully admit it might have seemed that I wanted you to be someone different. It wasn't you that was the problem though, and it took me a minute to wrap my head around the fact that maybe I was wrong."

"So, where does that leave us?" He flexed his hand like he wanted to reach for her but wouldn't allow himself to do so. "I can't change my background."

"I know."

"Do you?" He moved in closer. His scent was in her nose, and she wanted to bury her face against his chest. But they still had some things to work out. The sparkle had returned to his eyes, and she swallowed hard at his nearness. "Because you've held it against me a few times."

"I was letting my past with Clint cloud everything about my life. I measured everyone against the hurt he caused me, and I used the memory of that pain as a shield for why I had to protect myself, as an excuse for why I should stay alone."

"So, you're okay with me being a Wilder now."

"Yes," she said with a sigh. It had been unfair of her to hold his upbringing against him to start with. She'd just been unable to see past the wall of hurt Clint had built.

"Did you plan this new department to try to get me to stay in Woodvale?"

"Yes."

"You are going to marry me then." His mouth descended on hers before she could process his words and she returned his kiss with great enthusiasm. Electricity arced between them and warmed her quickly. Reluctantly, she pulled back though.

"We're at work," she said. "And did you just order me to marry you?"

"I'm not giving you a chance to say no." He nuzzled her cheek. "The last few weeks have been torture."

"You are too forgiving." She sighed, relishing the feel of his hands on her. "But can you please give me a chance to properly tell you just how sorry I am for hurting you?"

Swiftly, he leaned back, putting his hands behind his head. He looked so kissable that his actions didn't make it much easier to concentrate. She forced her eyes to his and focused on the apology she should have gotten out before allowing him to kiss her.

"I should have trusted you more." It still rubbed her wrong that she'd instantly assumed Beckett would run like Clint. But she had, and she'd let that fear control her and she'd nearly ruined the best thing that had ever happened to her as a result. "I'm really sorry that I didn't. And if it's any consolation, I've learned my lesson."

"Good." He brushed his fingers along her jawline. "I suppose since you've basically created a job just for me, I have to stay in Woodvale now, huh?"

"You've been wanting to get more ambulances in Woodvale, haven't you? I thought perhaps if I helped you accomplish that goal it would help you see that I'm truly on your side and supportive of you." She teased little circles on the smooth fabric of his suit pants. "I also think your talents are wasted here in this boardroom."

"Oh?"

She reached over and tugged his tie a bit. "I don't think these ties are quite right for you, are they? I'm dying to see you in an EMT uniform."

"And here I was wondering when I could get you out of some of your clothes."

"Beckett!" Her cheeks heated at his blatant flirting.

"It might not be easy, but I think if you're willing to give us a try, it will be worth it." He brushed the pad of his thumb over her lower lip.

"You were in cahoots with my dad about this, weren't you?"

"I needed to find a way for us to work this out. I realized it wasn't fair for me to ask you to give up your career when I wasn't willing to give up my house and this town. I needed to find a way to compromise." She shrugged. "Plan B was that Mason and I would follow you to Lexington."

"You were actually considering moving to be with me?"

"If that's what I had to do, then yes." A tear trekked down her cheek. "This will always be home for me, but you told me once that sometimes the people you are with can change how you feel about a place. Not having you here with me would make it hard to stay here now."

"I just have one question—are you keeping any other secrets from me?"

"Just one," she said softly.

"What's that?"

She wrapped her arms around his neck. "Only that I am in love with you, Beckett Wilder."

"I'm in love with you too, Jessamine Daniels."

EPILOGUE

One year later

JESS STOOD ON the back deck at the Wilders' lake house watching Mason try to teach Richard and Elaine about Pokémon. The expressions on their faces were a mixture of concentration and confusion. They had become active parts of Mason's life from the moment that Beckett had announced his engagement to Jess.

"Is he jabbering on about his Pokémon again?" Beckett asked as he walked up behind her.

"Oh, yes." She tilted her head and murmured in pleasure as his lips sought the pulse point on her throat that he knew drove her insane. "Where have you been?"

"Picking up a little something that I ordered for you."

"Hmm?"

He pulled out a small jewelry box. "Open it."

She took the proffered gift from his hand.

When she opened the lid, she found a small tornado charm on a delicate chain. "Oh…" she said, fingering the piece gently.

"It was one year ago today that the tornado hit Woodvale and threw you into my arms. We survived that storm by relying on each other, and I thought this might be a good reminder that if we lean on each other, we can survive any storm that life throws at us."

"I like that." She smiled broadly at him, trying her best to blink back tears. "Will you put it on me?"

She lifted her hair, and he fastened the clasp for her. "Should we go rescue them?"

"Nah. They can hold their own for a few more minutes, don't you think?" Beckett pulled her in for a searing kiss. It was several minutes before they ended the embrace.

"I suppose it wouldn't hurt for them to practice a bit before they become grandparents again in the fall." Jess looked up at him and waited for the news she'd just dropped on him to click.

"Are you telling me we are about to become a family of four, Mrs. Wilder?"

"I most certainly am."

Beckett put his hand tenderly on her stomach. "Really?"

She nodded. "You think Mason's going to want to be a big brother?"

"He's been asking for a brother since the day we got married—what do you think?"

"I think I am in awe at how much my life has changed in a year. I never imagined I could be this blissfully happy or that I could trust a man so implicitly again."

"You are the best thing that's ever happened to me too, Jess." His lips settled on hers again.

"Are y'all gonna kiss every minute of every day?" Mason asked, tugging on their arms.

"Only about seventy-five percent of them," Beckett teased. "The rest I'm going to spend chasing you and your brother or sister."

Mason had prepared to run, but Beckett's words froze him in his tracks. Confusion on his face faded to excitement. "A brother or sister? Really?"

Jess nodded. "Around Halloween."

"Sweet. Now I don't got to use my Christmas wish on a brother!" He ran away laughing.

"I told you he'd be happy."

"Dad, are you going to chase me or not?"

"I love hearing that." Beckett kissed her nose. "Dad… It never gets old. Now, if you will excuse me, love, I have a son to catch."

* * * * *